Rookie
of the Year

Rookie
of the Year

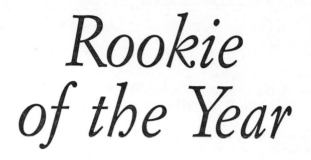

John R. Tunis
With an Introduction by Bruce Brooks

An Odyssey Classic • Harcourt, Inc.

ORLANDO AUSTIN NEW YORK SAN DIEGO TORONTO LONDON

www.HarcourtBooks.com

First Odyssey Classics edition 1990
First published 1944

The Library of Congress has cataloged an earlier edition as follows:
Tunis, John Roberts, 1889–1975.
Rookie of the year/John R. Tunis; with an introduction by Bruce Brooks.
p. cm.
"An Odyssey Classic."
Summary: Dodger manager Spike Russell's efforts to rally his team to
a pennant victory are threatened by a scheming club secretary and the
seeming irresponsibility of a star rookie pitcher.
[1. Baseball—Fiction.] I. Title.
PZ7.T8236Ro 1990
[Fic]—dc20   89-38710
ISBN-13: 978-0-15-205648-3   ISBN-10: 0-15-205648-3

Printed in the United States of America

H G F E D C B A

Introduction

John R. Tunis certainly had a thing about rookies. *The Kid from Tomkinsville* and *World Series* give us Roy Tucker's first year on the Dodgers, *Keystone Kids* follows Spike and Bob Russell as they come up together from Chattanooga to Brooklyn, and here we have the tale of Bones Hathaway, a lanky new pitcher for our beloved Brooklyn Bums.

It's easy to see why rookies were such attractive vehicles for Tunis's baseball stories. A major league baseball team is literally a *club*, with its own atmosphere, regulations, and social structure. It's a tough clique for a reader to crack; a newcomer can easily feel left out.

To avoid alienating the reader, some baseball writers bring the reader into a locker room that's more of a

Sunday School picnic than a clubhouse full of wary, competitive professionals. Veterans and stars all turn out to be really sweet fellows, ready to accommodate any intrusion. In the face of such a picnic, the reader may feel welcomed, but more likely he will feel humored. He will also miss the challenge of earning familiarity within an exclusive new world.

So, Tunis's trick is to leave the club as it should be—tough—but give the reader some company in the quest for admittance: another newcomer, a *character* in the story whose attempts to crack the club and learn the ropes are exactly what the *reader* needs to do. A real identification is established—almost a friendship between Roy or Spike and the reader. The action and atmosphere gradually reveal their mysteries to both reader and rookie; they learn together, sharing first their greenness and then their knowledge. The reader enjoys the extra thrill of feeling that the emerging hero of the book is his particular pal—"We've been together since the beginning."

Okay—but four rookie books in a *row*? Judging from the title alone, we might fear Tunis was in a rut. Fortunately, *Rookie of the Year* is quite different from the three rookie tales that preceded it.

Bones Hathaway, a rookie, is the Dodgers' star pitcher. This is quite a burden for a fresh kid. But it is not Bones's burden alone—in fact, he feels it rather less than the man who must depend on him the most: Spike Russell, kid manager. Spike, of course, became the manager in his second year as a Dodger; he is younger in years than all but a few of the Brooks, and it's clear that he likes counting on the older veterans to make his team click. Bones's immature antics upset Spike, and the manager makes an issue of them. Why, thinks Spike, why can't he be as wise as Fat Stuff or as cool as Roy?

But as the season rolls along, Spike needs to lean more and more on his immature star, even as his wrath with the kid grows. Then, in a marvelous bit of cruel irony, Bones makes a classy move to protect a friend from bad behavior, but is caught in a misunderstanding by Spike. The punishment is severe: He is cut from the team and sent home.

The irony plays itself out beautifully. Bones goes home with a clear conscience, while Spike is left with a fitful pitching staff and a team that has lost its fiery center, just as the pennant comes within reach. Spike's stubbornness bumps against his growing awareness that a wise man is a flexible man, until a little detective work gives him a way to forgive Bones and maintain his principles.

If *Rookie of the Year* were like the other Tunis rookie novels, we would stick with Bones, follow him home, wait for the call of forgiveness, sweat through his guilt or anger, and enjoy his redemption. But we don't go with Bones. We stick—for better or worse—with Spike. We fret and ponder and feel the dreadful weight of his decisions, sensing how every move affects the whole team, seeing the game suddenly from the broad angle of control.

This switch—from the easy identification with the rookie hero en route to stardom, to the troubled collaboration with the man in control—is a difficult move, but a great one. It's the move from innocence to experience, from playfulness to responsibility. Tunis is telling us we know enough now to play with the big boys and to understand them from the most sophisticated perspective. We don't need the crutch of the rookie-identity anymore; now a rookie is a gift and a problem.

However, as always, Tunis brings us along in perfect step with his characters. For if we are no longer able to hang out with the kids, it is only because he has forced us to move into an even tougher crowd, to join a more exclusive club. After four books, we have the savvy, the good humor, and the competitive edge to hang out with the likes of Razzle and Swanny and Elmer McCaffrey. We have arrived. We are *veterans*. It's a good feeling to know Tunis trusts us with the responsibility. We deserve it, just as we deserve the next Tunis novel, and the next, and the next. . . .

—Bruce Brooks

Rookie of the Year

1

The sun on the back of Spike's neck burned hotter than ever as he pawed restlessly at the dirt in the basepath and, leaning over, picked up a pebble nervously and tossed it behind him. Hands on knees, he glanced over his left shoulder at the row of goose eggs on the scoreboard.

This was the thing that made being a manager no fun. One of the things. You gamble on a kid pitcher in a tight spot. If he wins, he's a hero; if he loses, it's your fault.

Lots depending on that game, too. Not just beating the Cards, not trampling on the league leaders; but much more, the confidence necessary to make a rookie a regular, to give him the stuff to go on to other triumphs. Most of all, it meant the unity of the club, the team that was moving at last and only needed this victory to prove it to themselves. There they were, locked in a pitchers' battle, a scoreless tie going into the ninth, with no one out, two men on bases and the boy in the box showing signs of weakening for the first time.

Take him out or let him ride? This was surely one moment when being a manager wasn't fun.

"Alla time, Bones, alla time, Bonesy-boy . . ." From Spike's left came the sharp, shrill cry of his brother on second, and around and behind him familiar tones shouted reassuringly. It was a bad moment for the young pitcher, supported as he was by a rookie catcher. So much could happen and so quickly; one mistake in judgment, one ball where the hitter wanted it and bang! There goes the ballgame!

Bones Hathaway, the star rookie, straightened out the pitching holes before the rubber, shook off his catcher nonchalantly and, finally nodding, checked the men on bases and threw. A roar went up over the field. The batter turned, tossed away his bat, and started down toward first. The bases were filled and the next Card batter stalked briskly up to the plate. Spike, the young manager at shortstop, instantly realized the necessity for delaying things, for upsetting the batter's tempo and saying a word to his pitcher. From the corner of his eye he saw Rats Doyle and old Fat Stuff, his relief pitchers, working furiously in the bullpen. Yet the boy stood off the rubber, calmly rubbing up the ball with his bare hands as if it were a practice game in Florida.

When a manager goes out to the pitcher in a tight game, he's usually playing for time, and invariably asks the same questions. "How you feel? How's the arm?"

But Spike really wanted to know how the boy's finger was holding up. Early in the year this kid, who had come up from the minor leagues with a good record, had injured a finger on his pitching hand and lost the nail. That kept him out of play for weeks, and this was the first game he had pitched since that injury.

"Your finger O.K.? Lemme see." Spike inspected the boy's finger. "Any pain? All right, we'll get this one for you." He walked slowly back to his place. I'm gonna stay with him, he decided. I'm gonna stay with him. I believe the kid has what it takes.

Undisturbed by the noise round the park, the

boy stood motionless on the mound. He checked the runners, took the sign from the catcher, and shook his head. The crouching man behind the plate gave another signal; again the youngster in the box shook him off. Finally the catcher stood up. He came out to the mound and said something to his pitcher. Then he turned and came back again to the plate, while the runners danced off bases, the coaches yelled through cupped hands, and the crowd above roared.

Hang it all, Bonesy, throw him your hook, Spike thought. That baby is tough for a catcher to handle, no mistake. He's good, he knows he's good, but he wants his own way. And he can't be any fun to catch, either.

The batter swung on the first pitch. It was a comforting pop-up foul near first. Here's one of them anyway; there's a dead pigeon, thought Spike, as he watched the ball descend into Red Allen's mitt. That guy is sound; he's sure something to have around out there. Now for number two. I'm gonna stay with this kid.

The batter came to the plate, tapped it with his bat, touched his cap, glanced at his manager behind third for the hit or take sign. Would he bunt or hit away? The Dodgers were expecting a squeeze play, and as the arm of the pitcher went up Red Allen and Harry Street charged in from first and third. But the batter crossed them beautifully, hitting out and drilling a grasscutter past Red's outstretched glove.

From his place at second Spike watched anxiously as his brother Bob, the second baseman, dived for it, speared it, and pivoted all in one motion. Tense as he was, with the baserunner crashing down on him, he was stunned with admiration for the ease with which Bob made the play. No one else in the League could have pivoted that way or made that stop. The ball came to him low but hard; the man was out. One run was over, but there were two down.

He spit into his glove, leaned over and tossed some dirt behind him. Well, I was right to stick with this kid; he's a cool customer. What's more, he has a three-hitter now, and he deserves to win no matter what happens.

The batter waited while the boy on the mound arranged the dirt before the rubber, smoothed up the ball, looked round the bases, and did all the things a pitcher does in a tight place. It made the man at the plate nervous. He stepped from the batter's box, knocked the dirt from his spikes, and finally resumed his stance. From across the diamond came the confident chatter of the team behind their rookie hurler.

"Alla time, Bones. Alla time . . ." "Let him see it, Bonesy-boy, let him see your fast one. . . ."

Still throwing curves, the youngster, bearing down and coolly confident with two out, was soon ahead at two and one. At two and two the man hit. It was a blooper back of third. Spike started with the sound of the bat.

"Mine . . . mine . . . mine, Harry . . ." He had the angle, he had it, he caught it for the final out. Now they were running in together for the last of the ninth, one run behind.

Everyone was moving around the dugout, far too nervous to sit still; Swanny reaching for a towel to wipe his hands, Jocko Klein going over to the bat rack for his war club, Roy Tucker stepping up to the water-cooler. No one could sit quietly. They were standing, holding to the roof of the dugout, or kneeling on the step, or weaving in and out, talking to each other.

"Now, Jocko, put us back in there, kid. . . ." "Hey, Swanny, save me a rap. . . ." "C'mon, gang, le's go; le's get us some runs. . . ."

Spike heard the roar of the stands above. The crowds had been riding this rookie catcher until lately, and he wasn't sure what those cries above meant. He put one arm over the damp, heaving shoulder of his catcher.

"Never mind those wolves, Jocko. Never mind those wolves up there. You're my catcher. Go get us a hit." The dark-eyed boy nodded and stepped from the dugout to that trip to the plate.

He hit hard on the first pitch, a blow that had authority behind it, a blow that brought the whole dugout to the steps. But the Card center fielder, racing back, made a beautiful running catch over his left shoulder. Klein had rounded first and was well down toward second base when the fielder grabbed the ball off the fence.

Shoot! Shoot! Five feet one way or the other, and that would have been a ticket for third base. "Hard luck, Jocko; tha's hard luck; tha's really tough, kid. Now, Alan, keep us alive. Keep us alive in there."

Alan Whitehouse, a pinch hitter, responded by getting a clean single into right field. Immediately activity began out in the Cardinal bullpen. The Cards wanted the game, too. Swanson waited a couple of pitches and then hit a furious drive down the right field foul line, directly into the first baseman's mitt. Shucks, how's that for luck! Two blows that would both have been good for extra bases. If only that big boy hadn't been covering, Swanny would have made second standing up. Shoot, we can't seem to win anyhow!

Two out and a man on first. The activity in the St. Louis bullpen died away; quiet descended on the stands. But Red Allen was always a dangerous man, and the pitcher finally lost him. He trotted down to first and Roy Tucker, another bad actor with his bat, came to the plate.

Spike watched anxiously from the dugout step. We can do it; doggone, we can do it, we can still do it.

The pitcher was keeping the ball low, throwing to Roy's weakness. On the third pitch, the man at the plate dribbled a short, slow grounder toward short. He was off like a flash and so were the other two men on the bases. The throw was late, and now the bags were full.

Clyde Baldwin, a novice fielder, strode up. Two out, the bases full, and a freshman at bat! In the bullpen in deep left the St. Louis pitcher burned in a couple of last minute throws, and then came striding swiftly across the grass. The noise was tremendous now, the fans were all on their feet, so was the whole Brooklyn dugout. Even old Chiselbeak, who usually listened to the game over the Doc's radio in the lockers, was out there with a towel over his shoulders, calling for a hit, pleading with Clyde at the plate.

The Card third baseman came over and handed the ball to the incoming hurler. He stepped to the rubber, threw in a few warm-up pitches, and nodded to his manager. The three white-clad runners stood poised on base, the tying run on third, the winning run on second. Clyde tapped the platter twice, significantly. The Card short-stop turned, looked at the fielders, and waved them back. He knew Clyde as a long-ball hitter. When he leaned his hundred and eighty pounds behind a ball, it traveled.

The man in the box went carefully to work. The first pitch was low. Ball one. The crowd yelled. Clyde fouled the second into the stands. The third was low again. More shouts from the crowd. Only 180 feet from the plate, 180 feet from victory now; the winning run was perched there out on second base.

"C'mon, Clyde, c'mon, kid. Le's have the old stuff." "The big one left, boy, the big one left," shouted Bob at Spike's elbow. The entire dugout was yelling; no one heard, no one listened, the uproar around the field was continuous, the mob on its feet yelling for a run. "Over the fence,

Clyde, park one out there," they shrieked, while the pitcher, trying to take his time, stood astride the rubber taking the sign. He looked around the bases. Then he threw.

The pitch was low, just where Clyde wanted it, and he dumped a perfect bunt along the line and about a quarter of the way toward third, equidistant from the catcher, the pitcher, and the man covering the bag; the bunt, the smallest play in baseball, yet often the winning play.

Back deep on the grass the third baseman, caught by surprise, looked over at the pitcher and watched the ball trickle along. Right in that spot a bunt was the last thing he expected. It caught the pitcher, legs spread apart on the rubber, equally off balance. He also watched the ball dribble along the line, saw the third baseman was unable to make the play, and charged across. One run was over now, so, angry and flustered, he threw hurriedly to first. But Clyde was fast. He had passed the bag before the throw got there. The man on the base had to leap for it, and as he did so, Roy Tucker, speedster of the team, came roaring into the plate in a cloud of dust to score the winning run of the game.

2

Spike glanced over the crowded room. There's a difference, he thought, a big difference in this gang from last month. You can see it. Why, you can even feel it, too.

"Now, boys, we're really moving at last. That series with the Cards showed it, and I think maybe we opened their eyes to some things. They aren't the only ballclub in this League, they found out. We're starting to play like I knew all along we could, and I'm happier on lots of counts; think we're shaking down, think you realize we got a team that can go places if only we quit making mistakes. . . ."

A good baseball club is a continual challenge.

You can insult them into having pep and life if you're one kind of a manager; you can do it more subtly in different ways if you're another kind. Spike Russell was the other kind. He looked around at his team as he had often looked at them before, warm, familiar, friendly faces, at the men on the benches before their lockers or seated on the floor or standing up behind; at Jocko Klein, the Jewish catcher who because of his race had been the butt of the club—and other clubs in the League also; at Swanny, the big right fielder, with one arm carelessly over Jocko's shoulder; at his brother Bob spitting into his glove, impatient for action; at Clyde Baldwin, the freshman who was busting fences all over the League and making a name for himself as a ballplayer in left; at big Red Allen, the veteran first baseman, a comfortable man to have behind you in a pinch; at young Hathaway, the headstrong rookie pitcher, who was working slowly into form; at this team he had gradually fashioned from a disintegrating rabble.

"Yessir, I really think we can go places if we only quit making mistakes. If we don't beat ourselves. Reason the Yanks win is they never give a thing away. They score on your mistakes and they just never make any of their own.

"The team's in fourth place today. And we aren't moving backward, either. What's that, Raz?" The star pitcher, unable to resist the chance, was making a quiet crack to Roy Tucker at his side. But the alert young manager heard it and threw it right back at him. "The pennant? Well, we gotta chance. I haven't written that off yet. Sure we got a chance. Even if it is the first week in August, even if we are ten games back of the leaders. As long as we're in the League we gotta chance. . . .

"Now there's several things I'm gonna be strict about from now on. First of all, condition." He paused a moment, and turned his head to look at Bones Hathaway, the young pitcher, standing to one side. He wanted this to get home. "If you drink, and this applies especially to you pitchers, if you drink and stay out all hours of the night, you can't keep in condition. Get me? All of you get that? Now that brings up the second thing; hustle. Hustle and speed. You can all hustle, and I'm determined to get speed out of you. If we aren't a fast ballclub, we're nothing. We got Roy Tucker, about the fastest center fielder in the game. . . ." Murmurs of protest ran over the room.

"Yeah, that's right, that's correct. The fastest

man in baseball, Roy is. And Harry Street, and my brother there—why, he led the Southern Association in stolen bases several years ago. But we aren't grabbing them off the way we should. We gotta develop speed. 'S I say, if we aren't a speed club, we're nothing. I was looking up the records last night, and we're seventh in stolen bases. That's no good. From now on we'll start practice every day with a hundred-yard dash to the outfield, and then we'll run the same distance back again two minutes later. What's more, we'll run all out, everybody, me and every one of you. We'll practice hitting that bag with the left foot on the inside, same as we did last spring."

The room became silent. They could see their manager meant business. This was serious. He continued.

"I want speed, speed, and more speed; more hustle, too. I want you to run your hits out, run to your place in the field, run back to the dugout. I don't want to see any walking on this club from now on."

Man, he can really pour it on, thought his brother, seated before the locker with the big letters: RUSSELL, ROBERT, NO. 10, over it. He can sure pour it on, and they'll take it from him, too.

Why is that? It's because he's a good guy, because he's a real guy. He isn't one of these bench managers, getting fatter every day and running a club from the dugout. He does what he asks them to do; he's out there giving everything he has, same as the others. That's why they'll take it from Spike.

"Now we've got a vital three-game series with the Reds coming up. In my opinion, this Cincinnati team has no license to be ahead of us. They're just an ordinary, run-of-the-mill ballclub. Their new center fielder, Hutchings, is a pull hitter; watch that, Harry. They're not a fast club, so hurry them all you can. 'S I say, I want hustle and more hustle from every man on this team. They tell me when old John McGraw looked at a rookie he first asked him to run a hundred yards, then to bat, and last of all to throw. That's how important he considered speed." He hesitated a moment, and then started to name names.

"Clyde, the other day on that single there of Marshall's you didn't really hustle, you didn't give all you had, you didn't run hard enough. I don't want that to happen again. . . ."

"But, Spike, look-at," protested the fielder. "Look-at, there wasn't anyone on base at the time, and I fielded the ball clean on the third hop and held him to first. Didn't I?"

"Sure you did. You fielded it on the third hop instead of the second. If you'd run all out, you could easily have nabbed that ball on the second bounce. That might cost us a run some time, an important run; ever think of that? You're in the big time now, Clyde; keep your thinker oiled up every minute. And hustle. That's the chief fault, I b'lieve, in baseball—laxness in trying hard. Winning is the effect of nine men giving their best over a hundred and fifty-four games. In extra effort it means ten or fifteen games over the season. That's what I want, a team that plays heads-up ball every second. Bones, you're a good fielding pitcher; but you take too much for granted. Don't push your luck too far; some time you're gonna be sorry if you do. You other guys also. Now yesterday in the seventh, Swanny, you nabbed that foul out in deep right and the man scored from third. Nope . . . I'm not blaming you. I blame the boys in the bullpen 'cause nobody there called out. What's the matter, Rats? What's the matter with you and the rest of the boys in the bullpen? You're all part of the team; why weren't you hollering to Swanny on that play? Huh? Well . . . I guess that's about all. For now. This isn't any second division club, and I know if you'll hustle for me the way you can, we'll go places. Any questions?"

Raz Nugent raised one hand. Razzle, the big, brash pitcher who thought nothing of sneaking into the enemy clubhouse and listening in at their meetings, was just as bad in his own quarters.

"May I speak?" he asked politely.

The young manager beamed. He liked to have the men take part in the meetings. "Go ahead, Raz."

Razzle uncoiled his six feet two inches, and shuffled awkwardly to the front of the room. He yanked a sheet of white paper covered with figures from his back pocket. The room sat up with interest. The paper was evidently a list of the Cincinnati hitters and their weaknesses. They waited for Raz's comments, which they knew would be pungent, with interest.

Raz was a show-off. He stood looking around, feeling his audience with him.

"Now here's something that really has me stumped, Spike." He scratched his head, pushed his cap back on his brow, and glanced down at the paper in his hand. "The man at the garage soaked me $34.75 for fixing up my car the other day, and I think the bill is too darned high."

Spike gazed at him in stunned silence. Before he could intervene, a voice came from the group below. It was Rats Doyle, Raz's roommate and also a jokester.

"Naw . . . I don't hardly think that's overcharging, Razzle."

Raz nonchalantly shifted a huge lump of chewing tobacco in his mouth, and before he could adjust it to speak another voice chimed in.

"What did he fix, Raz?"

"There's a valve intake in the engine," explained the big pitcher, "that had to be repaired. But doggone, he's charging me for new parts, labor, and everything else 'cept the national debt. I think it's too much."

Immediately everyone in the room started to talk. Half the club thought it too high, others felt it was about right. But everyone had an opinion. Spike stood there listening to the argument for a moment. Finally he jumped in, bellowing at the top of his lungs over the din.

"QUIET! What the dickens has Raz's busted auto got to do with our beating the Reds this afternoon?"

Looking about the room, he perceived their

grinning faces. Then a momentary feeling of annoyance surged upon him as he noticed in the rear the familiar red face of big Bill Hanson, the club secretary. Bill's head was back, his huge frame shaking with laughter. Now Spike was angry at the older man. Hanson had no business snooping round at meetings for the team, and Spike started to say something. Then he suppressed his annoyance and decided to give Chiselbeak orders to keep Hanson out in the future. He collected himself, looked at the team, and being a smart manager, realized he was being taken for a mild sleighride. He threw his hands up.

"Meeting dismissed." He turned toward the door to the field amid a roar of laughter, shaking his head. Sure, they'd given him the bird, but just the same his heart was light. After all, they had as much right to ride him as Swanny or Rats or anyone else on the club. Wasn't he one of them? Of course. He was there on the field, dishing it out to the other clubs, yes, and taking it, too, with the rest of the team. Therefore he ought to be able to take it like the others inside the clubhouse.

He shook his head as they all clumped out the door, but secretly, in his heart of hearts, he was glad. Glad they felt they could ride him just the way they rode everyone else on the team.

Clack-clack, clackety-clack, clack-clack, clackety-clack, they stomped out to the field, laughing, talking, loose and happy. Yet not a team to be taken lightly because of those shouts and laughter, either.

3

Out around second base, the pivot base, that's the spot from which a ballclub can be sparked to life. Spike and Bob Russell, the Keystone Kids, were doing it, too, bringing fight and punch to the veterans flanking them, keeping everyone from getting sluggish. Age and youth, fire and experience; the combination was developing into a real infield, and the infield was fusing into a team. At first base was Red Allen, steady, dependable, always picking someone up with a brilliant stop or a catch of a wide throw. At second was Bob, a peppery wildcat through whom it was impossible to drive a ball; at third was Harry Street, a reliable veteran; at shortstop was Spike, hounding grounders like the lead dog in the sheriff's pack. That hot afternoon in early August the club came into Philadelphia treading on the heels of the Cincinnati Reds in third place, raring to go.

Spike could feel the looseness of his men by their gags and cracks as they warmed up around the dugout, while the home team took batting practice before the game. Familiar voices echoed about him. Over at one side three pitchers were warming up, Rats Doyle, young Hathaway, and old Fat Stuff Foster. Freddy Foster was too old to pitch often, so Spike seldom used him save for relief jobs or against the weaker clubs in the League. That afternoon he hoped to run him in, and stood there on the steps of the dugout watching the three men throw, wondering whether to spot his star youngster and make the game sure or save him for the tough Sunday doubleheader against the Cubs and take a chance with the veteran against the easier team. A decision hard to make; he put it off as long as possible. Guess right, and no one thinks anything about it; guess wrong, and you begin to lose the confidence of the management, the fans, and before long of your own men.

He stood on the step, wiping his forehead with

the sleeve of his sweatshirt. Then he heard the voice of Charlie Draper, one of the coaches, talking to a Philadelphia sportswriter.

". . . Yessir, that kid really has what it takes. He's a cool customer. Y'know, only the other day over at St. Loo, the Cards got three men on in the ninth, and Danaher comes up with two out. Jocko Klein gives Bonesy the sign for a fast ball. The kid shakes him off. So Jocko gives him the sign for a hook, and the boy shakes him off again. Jocko, he walks out to the box. 'What's the matter, young fella?' he says. 'Don't you *want* to pitch?' "

The reporter laughed. Suddenly he observed Spike standing alone on the dugout step, eyeing his pitchers in the act of warming up. The newshawk walked across. "Hullo, Spike, how's tricks?"

"Fine." Spike kept his gaze on the three men throwing to the catchers. He always remembered what Grouchy Devine, the manager of the Volunteers when he and Bob had been in the Southern League, used to say. "When you don't talk, you don't never have to eat your own words."

"Say, this kid Hathaway looks good. He

oughta beat some clubs in this League with that sinker."

"Yeah. He's gonna help us plenty."

"That win over the Cards last week won't hurt. I understand he pitched real ball."

"He'll do better next time."

"He must have been hot the other day, though. The Cards were here the next afternoon; they said they couldn't see his fast one."

"Yeah. Well, he'll improve."

"Those Cards said his fast one has a mean hop to it."

"If all you can throw is fast balls, it's murder," said Spike succinctly.

"Yeah? Oh, yeah, of course. But he's got a hook, too, a major league curve, and a big time pitching delivery. But that fast ball . . . funny. I was just out there watching him. He's not a big boy; why, he's almost slender."

"Yes, but he's got a good chest and he gets his shoulders behind the ball. See . . . see there. . . ." Silence for a moment, while they stood side by side watching the youngster pour it in.

"Uhuh. He breaks his stuff low."

Bill Hanson's voice broke in. "He'll be a swell pitcher all right, if only he'll lay off the beer."

Spike turned. Hanson again! Now who asked him to give out with his two cents' worth? The young manager had the soldier's half-expressed contempt for the non-combatant. He turned his back on the club secretary and addressed the sportswriter directly.

"Lemme tell you something. That kid's arm went bad last year; he wasn't even taken down to spring training camp. So whad' he do? He goes to Montreal, played the outfield, developed into quite a pinch hitter in a short while, too. Was batting around two ninety. 'I won't quit,' he told Buz Farrell up there. 'Nope, I won't quit base-ball 'cause I love it. They may chuck me out; but I won't quit.' So Buz stayed with him, and after a while the boy tried pitching again. His arm came back and he won six straight games, so we called him down about a month ago from Montreal. First game he stopped a liner with his meat hand and lost the nail of one finger. That set him back quite some time, 'bout two-three weeks. But now he's coming along. He's a pitcher, now."

Spike Russell seldom talked as much as that to outsiders. For a moment he forgot he was addressing a sportswriter. Then he turned away as the umpires gathered around home plate.

Ten minutes later he was sitting beside Fat Stuff while the Dodgers were taking their raps. Whenever possible the young manager sat beside his old hurler, never failing to learn something valuable. The old timer had a knuckle ball, a screw-ball, control, the whole tempered with aggressiveness. Best of all, he had a thorough knowledge of the hitters. Together, manager and pitcher discussed Danny Lee, the home-run slugger of the last place Phils.

"If only we can handcuff that guy, this team is a pushover, Fat Stuff."

The old fellow nodded. "Yeah. You know he strikes out prob'ly more than anyone in the National League; but he's a darn dangerous man in a tight spot. And he's bad medicine for the lefties; glad I pitch right-handed."

"Yeah, he really owns the lefties, doesn't he? How you plan to throw to him, Freddy?"

"Well, he's a loosey-goosey at the plate. Thing to do is to avoid giving him that letter-high fast ball across the middle. He hits that one out of sight. Two years ago in the All-Star game in the Yankee Stadium, I seen him belt one of Royal Davis' pitches clean out into the bullpen in deep center. Boy, that's a good bit over four hundred and fifty feet. Yessir, he can paste it. Well now, you can throw to Danny Lee four ways to get him out. The spots to pitch to him are: high, inside; high, outside; low, inside; low, outside. Oh . . . say . . . looka that catch! Roy was robbed that time. That's tough, Roy." Fat Stuff picked up his glove, shifted his wad in his mouth, hitched at his pants, and went out to the mound to go to work.

The game was close from the start. Few men got on base; those who did died there. The Brooks were hitting hard but right at the fielders, hits that didn't mean a thing. The Phillie pitcher was stingy, and as the game progressed they kept returning scoreless to the bench after each inning.

"Say . . . aren't you boys going to get me any markers?" complained the old pitcher. "Hey there, what's the matter with you guys?"

Spike became almost ashamed, watching the veteran pitch his heart out, putting the opposing side down in short order at the plate, yet still without a run to win. Finally, in the eighth, they managed to squeeze across one tally. Fat Stuff squelched a rally in the last of the eighth himself, with a beautiful stop of a hard hit ball to the left of the box. Finally they came into the last half of the ninth, still clinging to that precarious lead. Two men went down in routine fashion. The Brooks peppered the ball around the infield, chattering at Fat Stuff, everyone thinking of those cooling showers, of dinner, and the end of a hard, hot day. Then the third batter hit a long, lazy single.

The sparse crowd, scattered throughout the huge stadium at Shibe Park, now paused at the exits and began to come to life. Fat Stuff went to work on the next batter. He's careful now, thought Spike, he's throwing careful to get this man. Actually, the veteran pitched far too carefully and lost him, giving up his first base on balls of the game. Plain to see the old pitcher was tiring. The next batter topped a slow ball toward third and beat out Harry Street's throw by a foot. Three on, last of the ninth, and Danny Lee, the club's heavy hitter, strode to the plate while the home crowd yelled. This was the big moment.

Spike looked anxiously at the bullpen where Rats Doyle and Rog Stinson were burning in their throws. Then he glanced back at old Fat Stuff, standing quietly on the mound in that din of noise and clap-clapping from the stands. Shall I yank him? No, siree! I'm gonna stay with him. He's pitched one swell game, and he's the foxiest man I've got in a spot such as this. Besides, it'll show the kids like Hathaway that I stay with my pitchers; it'll build up that lad's confidence in himself. . . .

The first ball was high, inside, and Danny Lee swung under it a foot, so hard he swung right off his feet. The swing checked the noise in the stands abruptly. The next pitch was high, outside. The batter looked at it, and now the count was even at one and one.

The roar over the half-empty ballpark resumed. From his position in deep short, playing for a force-out at second, Spike watched Jocko Klein's signal. The veteran shook the kid off. He took the next signal and nodded. The ball was going low; low, inside. The batter took his cut, only got hold of a piece of it, and fouled it into the stands. One and two. Again the old chap was ahead of the man at the plate.

Then something made Spike turn to glance at the scoreboard, and he saw the figures on the game in Cincinnati; Chicago, 3, Cinci, 1. The Dodgers would be in third place! One more pitch, one more good pitch and we're in third, and we won't look back, either. C'mon now, Fat Stuff. One more pitch. "Lay it in there, boy;

O.K., now. . . . Let him see it, Fat Stuff . . . old kid, old boy . . . alla time now, alla time. . . ."

Without any wind-up the veteran threw. It was low, outside, and would certainly have been called a ball had the home-run hitter of the Phils not swung at it, swung well over it for the third strike. High, inside; high, outside; low, inside; low, outside. Three strikes and the game was over!

The Dodgers were in third place. Their highest standing of the season. Triumphantly they rushed for the showers, jubilant at having won and pulled up from sixth to third. Now the team was moving at last. Spike found himself trudging along beside Charlie Draper, the coach, his jacket slung over his shoulder, the leather ball-bag in one hand. The coach knew baseball. He shook his head in admiration at the veteran's canny pitching.

"Yessir, he really has what it takes, that man Foster, he really has. Y'know, Spike, this would be quite a ballclub if everyone hustled same as old Fat Stuff."

Spike looked quickly around. He hoped some of the young pitchers heard that crack.

"It sure would," he agreed.

4

A week later Spike was seated in a taxi in Chicago on the way from the hotel to Wrigley Field with Bill Hanson, the club secretary, and Charlie Draper, the coach. Spike went back to the game of the previous afternoon. "Shoot! We never should have lost that one yesterday. Made me mad!"

"Me, too. It was a tough one for Bones Hathaway to lose," rejoined Charlie. "He pitched first-class ball. Why, he was flipping little peas to those Cub batters. His fast ball was right pert."

"Yeah," said Spike, "the kid has it. He has the know-how of pitching. What I like about him is his stance after he's thrown, both feet planted firmly before him in perfect fielding position."

"He's one of the best fielding pitchers I've ever seen," said Hanson sagely. "The best since Snicker Doane of the Yanks." Hanson had been around baseball for years, and always harked back to an era in the game no one else could remember. Consequently no one could ever contradict him. "He's gonna help this club plenty, if he'll only let the liquor alone."

"He'd better," replied the young manager firmly. "He'd better unless he wants some thin salary checks coming up. What time's the train for St. Loo leave tonight, Bill?"

"Six-thirty. Don't go into extra innings. Shall we give the boys dinner money?"

"Uhuh. Give 'em dinner money." Spike went back again to the game of the previous afternoon. "So help me, Charlie, we should never have dropped that one."

Although he addressed the remark to Charlie on his left, it was Hanson, somewhat to Spike's annoyance, who answered. "Nope. Here we are in the second week in August. Doesn't look too good, does it?"

Now Spike really was annoyed. Sometimes he

wondered whether Hanson was for him or against him. But he knew that all club secretaries thought they knew more baseball than any of the players, so he controlled himself and answered courteously. "Bill, I'm afraid you don't know your baseball history. D'ja ever hear of the 1921 Giants winning after being seven and a half games behind in late August? Or the Yanks blowing a 13-game lead in 1928, and just barely limping home? Or the 1935 Cubs staging a 21-game, late-season winning streak? Or the Pirates building a World Series press box in 1938 that was never used? Or the Cards catching the Dodgers from ten games back in August, 1942, and . . ."

"Maybe you got something there, Spike, maybe you got something there. I just meant . . ." Hanson was the sort of person who agreed with anybody who put up an argument. But Spike wished to squelch that defeatist talk. It could hurt the club badly.

"If you're trying to hint to me the outlook is dark, I say nuts to all that, Bill. I know baseball history. I haven't been round as long as you have but I've seen enough to know this team won't stop until they flash the mathematics on us. I never said we'd win the pennant. I don't go in for predictions. I only said we gotta chance. I said that back in June, when we were hanging on to seventh place; I said it in July when we were fifth; and I say it today when we're third. Yes, even if we did drop an important one yesterday."

"Yeah . . . yeah . . . oh, yeah, that's right. You're dead right, Spike. . . ."

Charlie Draper felt the atmosphere tighten. He spoke up. "We needn't have lost that game yesterday at all if young Baldwin hadn't gone into third standing up in the sixth. Too darned lazy to hit the dirt, he was. Went in standing up, so he was out; then Klein hits that double which would have won us the game. Spike, it's what you were saying the other day, the effect of nine men giving their best over a hundred and fifty-four days; that means ten or fifteen games, that extra effort."

How to get this extra effort, how to make each player come through with his best all the time, which man to drive, which to coax along, which to holler at, that's the job of the manager. That's my job, thought Spike, looking out the taxi window. "Charlie, I like to kill that kid right there on the spot before the crowd. I was so mad I couldn't speak to him last night. I did this morning, though. I had breakfast with him and told him a few things. 'That cost us a mighty important game, boy, and it's gonna cost you fifty bucks,' I told him."

"How'd he take it?"

"How could he take it?"

"Just the same, Spike, the team's rolling better since you traded Case and stuck in this boy there in left field. Y'know, Case was a trouble-maker."

"Sure," Hanson spoke up. "Karl Case was the one who started all that name-calling with Jocko Klein. Look at Jocko now. What a ballplayer he turned out to be."

"Always was," said Spike sharply. "He always was a ballplayer. And the way he backs up with men on base is just something. I bet he saved us three different times in tight spots yesterday."

"Doggone, then that dopey kid Baldwin has to go and lose it for us. Shoot, we would have picked up a whole game on the Cards. The Pirates, too."

"Raz Nugent says we lost yesterday because he hasn't got locker 13." Hanson grinned. "Says we always lose in this town when he hasn't got locker 13. He's trying the worst way to get Harry Street to change, and Harry won't, 'cause he went three for five the other day and wants to hang onto that number."

"These birds are sure funny," said Draper. "D'ja ever notice Roy Tucker at bat? When he first comes up he always taps the four corners of the plate."

"Yeah, an' Jocko Klein always puts his left shoe on first."

"An' Fat Stuff, if he wins a game he wears the same inner socks until he loses; why, he'll wear 'em until they fall off him."

"Remember that trick of Razzle's, the way after every inning he chucks his glove across the foul line ahead of him, then when he reaches it, leans over and moves it so the fingers point toward third base? Well, I was asking him about that the other day. He says there's folks stop him on the street and question him; says they come out to the ball park just to see him do it."

"That big guy'll slay me," remarked Hanson. "Over in Cinci he got hold of a pair of rabbits and kept them four days in his room in the Netherlands Plaza. They ate up four square yards of rug. The hotel people like to throw us all out of the place. I made Raz pay for it though, every red cent."

The taxi drew up at the side entrance to the

field. Spike stepped out, and instantly the trio was assaulted by a mob of kids.

"Hey, Mr. Russell . . . give us yer autograph. . . . Mr. Russell, will ya. . . please. . . ."

5

Bill Hanson was in the grill of the Coronado drinking a highball with Jim Casey of the *News*. Casey had listened to the game that afternoon on a portable radio he had carried into the press box, and was describing the linguistics of Snazzy Beane, the remarkable St. Louis broadcasting genius. Now Casey was giving a fairly good imitation of him.

"He goes into his act something like this. 'He's rounding second . . . the bases are cleared . . . he's going into third . . . folks, he's did it! He slud into third for a triple!'"

Hanson threw back his head. He laughed. His red face became even redder. "Say, no human being but Snazzy Beane could take the verb 'slide,' call it 'slud,' and make it mean the same thing. Only more so."

"It's a fact," replied Casey. "Look. Who's that girl over there . . . at the table with—who is it? Why, it's Hathaway and Baldwin!"

"Where? Which one?" Hanson instantly stood on the rung of his stool at the bar and looked carefully over the noisy, smoke-filled room.

"There! That table in the corner, there." The noise of pounding came from one end of the room, and above the din could be heard Hathaway's strong tones.

"Waiter! Waiter!"

Then he saw them. They were at a corner table with a girl in red. Yes, it was Hathaway and Baldwin, the rookie roommates. He recognized the girl, too, for Hanson had been around. "Why, sure, that's Jane Andrews, the gal who sings at the Club Royal. I understand Baldwin knows her; they both come from the same town somewhere down in Tennessee."

The men at the bar watched with interest. The ballplayers were noisy, and the room was watching them. Before long everyone seemed to be aware of the fact that a couple of the Dodgers were back there with a girl at the corner table.

Casey after a minute resumed his account of the broadcast of the afternoon's game.

". . . Well, Bill, in the seventh the guy goes wild. You remember, when they scored that tying run. 'Folks,' he says, 'folks, I just wanna tell you one thing. This is . . . the nuts. Yes, sir . . . the nuts. I'm a-broadcasting to you about the greatest team in baseball, and when the World Series comes, they'll run them Yankees clean out of the park.'"

"Yeah, he's something, isn't he? Tommy Holmes sat next to him one afternoon in the broadcasting booth. He said it was like being at a doubleheader; you saw one game and heard another."

Casey glanced up. The yells for the waiter from that table in the corner increased. "Those boys had better watch out. If Spike Russell catches Hathaway down here two days before he's gotta pitch, he'll peel his hide off him."

"Aw, Russell thinks he knows everything there is to know about baseball. Why, I was connected with baseball before he was dry behind the ears," said Hanson.

Casey, watching the trio in the corner, made no reply. The whole room was looking at them now. Then he turned back to the bar and his half-finished drink.

"What was I saying? Oh, yes, Snazzy Beane. Well, then, in the sixth, when they threw Baldwin out at third, he really winds up. 'Say, folks, do you suppose they broadcast these games to Flatbush? If they do, them folks can't be enjoying their dinner much. I'll say. An' we ain't gonna stop winning, either. We'll belt that boy Hathaway right off the mound next Monday night, you see if we don't. He beat us in Brooklyn; but he won't repeat, you take it from ol' Snaz. We're in, folks, and you can call up them Yanks and tell 'em that for Snazzy!'"

The commotion at the corner table became louder as chairs scraped and the three rose and came toward the bar. They were singing, all of them.

"She's gonna cry . . . until I tell her that I'll never roam . . . Chattanooga choo-choo . . . won't you take me back home . . . home . . . home . . ."

They pushed and shoved their way past the crowded bar to the stairs. Jim Casey, ever sensitive to a news break, shoved half a dollar on the bar and disengaged himself from his stool. Without a word to Hanson he trailed the three singers to the doorway as they staggered upstairs. Arm in arm, they emerged into the lobby and reached the elevator just as the door opened with a bang and Charlie Draper followed by Spike Russell stepped out.

The manager took one look. He turned without speaking and walked into the Coffee Shoppe. The veteran coach was at his heels.

By morning everyone knew it, for a thing of this kind spreads fast on a ballclub. So no one was surprised the next day when a meeting was called. But this was not an ordinary meeting. Only the team was present; outsiders were excluded. Doc Masters wasn't there, and the players noticed that Chiselbeak held the door open while the two coaches stepped through, and then kept Bill Hanson from entering. They looked at each other. Certainly this was no ordinary meeting.

"Now there's just one thing I want to bring up this afternoon." The room was painfully quiet. Aha, so he's going into that! Yep, that's it!

Spike paused and glanced around; at his brother in the group at his feet; at the others, most of them dark and tanned, a few like Swanson who was blond and never seemed to tan no matter how much he stayed in the sun. But

Bob and Swanny and all of them were tired and drawn about the eyes. They were solemn and serious, too. They knew what the meeting was about.

"I'll get right to the point. I want . . . nobody . . . on this club . . . touching liquor. Hope that's understood." How can you say it more simply? How can you get it over to them that I really mean business, that what I'm saying is no joke? He looked at the men on the benches before him, sitting about the floor or leaning against the lockers. His face was hard. He hesitated, holding the two rookies, Hathaway and Baldwin, in his glance, addressing them directly. "If any of you boys, and that means any of you, feel you must . . . that is, if you feel booze is necessary . . . well . . . get out!" The last words came savagely. Heads all over the room went up. The men leaning casually against the lockers suddenly straightened. "If liquor is necessary, go to some other team; don't stay here. There's some things a few managers overlook. I can't. I don't want you if you drink; don't care how swell a guy you are; don't care if you bat .400 or win me twenty-five games a year. I don't want you. If you stay, if you stay and start drinking, and I catch you . . ." His voice dropped but it lashed through the quiet room. ". . . If I catch you, and I will catch you as sure as sure . . . I'll fine you fifty bucks the first time, and a hundred the second. There's two men on this club know already I'm not fooling."

The silence that lasted, painful in its length, was broken as usual by Razzle. No matter how serious the moment, the brash prima donna of the team had to inject his personality. "How 'bout the third time, Spike?"

There could have been titters, laughter even. But before the team's mood could change, Spike jumped. He turned quickly toward the big pitcher standing against a locker to the side. There was anger in the sudden movement of his body, anger in his voice and his quick words. Everyone connected with the club from Mac-Manus down treated Raz with the respect that his salary, his reputation, and his pitching record deserved. Spike Russell was different. He forgot all that. To him Raz was just another player. And for once the showboat of the squad regretted his remark. For once he was not to enjoy holding the center of the stage.

"Razzle! There isn't . . . there won't be any third time. For you or anyone else on this club." He spoke as if he meant it and he did. They realized their manager was in no light mood. "I may lose my pitching staff. O.K. I may risk the pennant. O.K. again. I may even break up this club. O.K. If you're a drinker . . . you're through as far as I'm concerned. That means you, too, Raz, same as everyone else. Baseball's a business. If business interferes with your drinking, go where it doesn't.

"What's the reason I'm tough about this? It isn't the usual reasons. This is no Sunday School; we're a ballclub, not a reform school. Even a few beers now and then slow a man up; he don't get that extra step in beating out a bunt or stealing second, or that burst of speed he needs to nab a low drive in the field or grab it one hop sooner. That's all true enough, but that's not all there is to it. The point is this . . . a drinker . . . only one drinker . . . can ruin a club and its pennant chances, too. My brother Bob and me learned this a long while ago and it cost us plenty."

Now there was a slight rustle over the room; a cough in the rear, the scrape of a spike across the floor, the noise of a bench creaking as someone shifted. Yet they watched him closely, they listened carefully as he continued.

"Back some years ago we were a couple of

utility outfielders on the Dallas Rebels in the Texas League. 'Bout halfway through the season several of the boys got banged up, and Rhodes, the manager, shoved us in at second and short. We were only kids and we took quite some knocks; but we hung on, we played ball, and toward the end of the season the club finished third and was in there fighting in the play-offs for the Dixie Series against Beaumont. Night before the deciding game, a scout from the Pirates came to see us. Said he liked our looks and might send us along with Buster Reynolds, our star southpaw, up to the Syracuse Chiefs, their farm in the International League.

"There was our chance. We couldn't believe it. Buster, now, he was plenty hot that season. He'd won seventeen for us and looked good. He met this scout the same evening, and afterward he thinks: 'I'm as good as in the big time; I've made the grade,' he thinks. 'I'll just loosen up and have me a beer.' He did. Had several. Next day Beaumont scored six runs and knocked him out of the box in the first inning. We never got a chance in the field until the scout had quit in disgust. The final score was eight to nothing. Buster didn't go to the Chiefs that next year; neither did we.

"We figured we were through 'cause Buster Reynolds went haywire that night. We weren't. But it was a long road up; a couple of years with Scranton in the Eastern League, then for a while with Little Rock in the Southern, until we were traded to Nashville and Grouchy Devine. Three-four years all on account of that bender of Buster Reynolds'. We lost the pennant, we lost the Dixie Series, and a lot of time into the bargain. So . . . you'll understand why I mean business about liquor on this club."

There was silence again. Everyone was thinking the same thing—of men they'd known; of Mike Stanley of the Cubs, who ruined his career and ended up as a grounds-keeper in Cinci; of that kid Beichman on the Senators, who was let out in the middle of the season; of old Jeffers, the veteran lefty, who couldn't hold on in any league; of a dozen others who had suddenly disappeared, dropped out, lost to baseball, never heard from again. That's what they were all thinking.

"So it's no drinking. That means . . . *no* drinking. I don't know how I can make it any straighter. I don't know how I can prove to you I mean business . . . except to say you've been warned, everyone on this club. Is that plain? Do you get me? I want no excuses, nobody saying they didn't know . . . they didn't understand . . . they didn't think I meant it that way."

This time even Razzle was quiet. No one dared look at Hathaway and Baldwin in front. No one stirred. No one moved and the room was silent. Spike Russell reached back in his hip pocket for his glove.

"Meeting dismissed!"

6

Ballplayers dislike night games. For one thing, night games mean sitting around a hotel lobby all day waiting to go out to the park. Movies? Take in a movie and you'll tire your eyes in no time. For another thing, night games interfere with a man's regular meals. A player likes to have a big dinner after he has finished, but if the game is at night, he must eat in the late afternoon, beforehand, and must have a light meal. Moreover, if the contest goes into extra innings, he won't be able to leave the grounds until after eleven o'clock. Then he can't get to bed until after midnight and perhaps isn't relaxed enough to sleep before two or three in the morning. Often he has to rise early to catch a train; in any event his rest is upset. And while lighting in the majors is excellent and visibility good, the smoke pall which hangs over the park in the evening mist is hard on the eyes and makes them smart all the next day.

Yet night baseball is dramatic. The vivid lights give the grass a peculiar emerald color, the uniforms are a brilliant white, the colors all sharpened. And the fans like night games, especially in certain cities. St. Louis is one of them.

They came early that evening; it was daylight when they started pouring into Sportsman's Park; they came in the dusk; they swarmed in as twilight settled and the batting cage was placed round the plate and the players took hitting practice. Long before the umpires appeared, the bleachers in right and center were jammed and the double-decked stands back of first, third, and the plate were filled. The crowd packed the stadium; the general tenseness in the air gave the game almost a World Series feeling. By now the Cards saw a dangerous contender in the Dodgers and were determined to win. While the Brooks, beaten the day before, wanted revenge from the League leaders.

This was the setting into which Spike Russell threw his star freshman, Bones Hathaway, a tough spot for the youngster. Naturally he was nervous at the start. In the first inning the Cards threatened to tear the ballgame apart. Three straight singles scored a run, and Spike waved to the bullpen for action. He always signaled with his right arm for a right-hander and his left arm for a lefty. This time he waved for Rats Doyle, a left-hander and a man he liked to throw in early when necessary. It wasn't necessary. Before Rats could get properly warmed up, the batter looked at a third strike, and Bob and Spike took young Hathaway out of a hole with a quick doubleplay ball.

From then on he settled down, pitching brilliant baseball. For many long innings not a Redbird got as far as second. In the sixth the Dodgers pushed over a run and tied the score when Allen doubled, was sacrificed to third, and came in on Clyde Baldwin's long fly to deep left field. The seventh, the eighth, the ninth, and both hurlers seemed to get better the longer they threw. The tightness increased. The crowd howled and shrieked for a run, clap-clapped and hooted to rattle the youngster in the box, cheered and roared when a Card was walked, groaned and settled back when the next two men struck out and the side was retired. In the tenth, with one down, Bob banged a liner over second base, and Jocko Klein, told to hit, did hit. When the fielder got the ball back there were men on second and third and a score threatening.

The Card infield came in on the grass. A situation like this, with a man on third and one out, is the best situation in baseball for the offensive team. The defensive infield is obliged to play in, making it easier for the batter to hit through them, and adding about fifty feet to the acre of ground in which a Texas leaguer can fall safely. Also a run may be scored on a long fly ball.

The whole set-up screamed for a squeeze play; the stands expected it, so did the Cards. But Spike crossed them up. He ordered Swanny to hit away. Stein, the Card pitcher, was crowding him all the time, pitching tight to his weakness, a high inside ball. Instead of pounding it hard, Swanny only got a piece of it and poked one up in the air near second. The ball disappeared in the haze and smoke of thousands and thousands of cigars and cigarettes. It went up, up, out of one light zone into another, appearing and disappearing and then descending into the glove of the waiting shortstop. Two out!

Shoot! Shucks, that's bad! "All right, Red, pick us up now; save us, Red, old timer; we gotta get this man over. Hit that ball."

Red hit. A long ball deep to the right side. The runners were off with the sound of the bat and Red rounded first and was well down toward second when the Card fielder, running a country mile, made a desperate one-handed stab of the ball almost in the stands in right.

The eleventh went past without a score. So into the twelfth and thirteenth. The clock showed almost midnight now, yet not a seat emptied, not a fan moved from the park. A scratch hit put the first Card batter in the fourteenth on base and he was promptly sacrificed to second. A man on second and one out; a dangerous situation with the boy in the box tiring and the stands above shrieking for a hit. Then in deep short, Spike, with one eye on the active bullpen and another on the runner before him on the path, caught Jocko Klein's signal. He was wiping his mitt across his chest nervously. That meant a throw to pick the man off second on the third pitch.

At first Spike didn't believe it, thought the motion was merely a nervous gesture. One bad throw and there's the ballgame and you're the goat, Jocko, the all-time goat. But he did mean it. He gave it again. All signs must be answered by the fielder to make sure he receives them, and as the batter fouled off a strike into the stands Spike flashed the signal in return. On the second pitch now.

The first pitch was low, inside, a ball. The crowd howled with delight, little knowing what was taking place down there on the field before their eyes. A cool customer, this kid Hathaway, thought Spike. He's setting the batter up so he'll be looking for a fast ball on the next one. And Jocko Klein, he's cooler still. He's really got nerve, that boy. Well, here we go!

There were six steps in this play. First Spike's sudden burst toward second; the piercing yell of the coach behind third; the runner's realization of his peril; his dive back to safety; the catcher's throw to the base; and last the catch and tag done about simultaneously. It was the fourteenth inning, and because the runner was tired his reactions were more sluggish than usual. The pitch-out was perfect, shoulder high and well away from the man at the plate, just where Klein wanted it. The catcher let go with everything he had. The runner was a second slow in moving back. Spike got the ball on the outside of the bag and slapped it on him as he tried desperately to slide to safety.

Two minutes later they were running in to the bench. Spike overtook the stocky catcher walking wearily along, his mask in his hand. "Boy, you really got what it takes, Jocko. Two feet the other way and that ball would have been out in center field and you'd have been the goat of the series. Pull us out of a rally like that and you pull us back into the game, and that wins pennants." They came into the bench. "Now, gang, le's us get some runs for Bonesy."

But they couldn't seem to get runs. Neither could the Cards. The fifteenth went by without a score. In the sixteenth the Keystone Kids saved their young pitcher again with a quick double-play after he passed a man. In the seventeenth the game seemed lost. The first batter worked another base on balls. The next man, attempting to bunt, popped in front of the plate to Jocko Klein. Then the third man came through with a deep hit to the flagpole in center field, and before Roy Tucker could get his hands on it there were men on second and third and only one down.

Bones teamed up with Red Allen to retire the

next batter who tried to squeeze the runner home. It was a roller down the third base line, but short, and the pitcher fielded it perfectly, holding the man on the bag and then making a quick throw to Allen, who tagged the runner just as he came in with a crash to first. Now all Hathaway had to do was get the shortstop, a weak hitter.

The thing came with the suddenness of disaster. Not a clean hit, not a solid blow as a fitting end to that endless struggle, but an easy ball, a topped roller near the plate, not more than twenty feet from Klein. With two out, both runners were off immediately. So was Bones Hathaway, the best fielding young pitcher in the League. He rushed in on top of the ball, scooped it up, and as he did so his spikes failed to catch, and his feet went out from under him. No need to look toward first, for he could make no play there, so in a last despairing try he fired the ball at Klein, astride the plate for just such an emergency. The throw, made from a sitting position, was low and wide. The runner slid in and the game was lost.

For a second Spike, anxiously watching, hoped there might be a chance the runner had missed the plate in the mix-up. He dashed in, grabbed the ball, and tagged him. But Stubble-beard, the umpire, shook his head, and turning his back departed for the dugout tunnel to the dressing room. The game was over. The Dodgers had lost three straight, and the Cards had increased their lead over the second-place Pirates.

7

They fought their way through the frenzied fans and trooped in to the lockers, sore, tired, silent. No one said much. There wasn't much to say. For once even Razzle Nugent was gloomy and quiet. No one talked; everybody slumped down exhausted on the hard benches in the hot room, realizing how the effort of climbing into third place had taken its toll of nervous energy, how weary and beaten they were. No one rushed to the showers, no one even undressed, there was no singing or shouting or horseplay. Numbness and disappointment hung over the entire room.

Boy, is that a tough one to lose! Spike sat

beside his brother, speechless like the others. Gee whizz, six chances and no hits! No, seven chances; nothing for seven. Maybe I swung too hard. 'Member that long hit the first game; I choked my bat, that's what I should have done again. Walked once, hit on the arm once, and five times without a thing to show for it. That's no way for a manager to act. This isn't, either, sitting here letting those boys worry their hearts out. Spike climbed up on his bench and stood there.

"Look here, you guys. We lost one to the League leaders, so what? When a fella pitches ten-hit ball over seventeen innings like Bones just did, he's hot. I'll say. After all, we're only seven games out of first as it is, and we're still fixed in third, and back there in June we'd have settled for third place any day, you all remember that. Now don't worry over this game. You gave me all you had, every single one of you, you played heads-up baseball. Just forget this and let's go get those Pirates over in Pittsburgh. Take those wet things offa you now and have yourself a good shower."

Gradually they peeled off their soggy clothes and moved to the showers, feeling the voluptuous caress of steam spray on tired backs, aching arms, and weary legs, shaking the soothing wetness off their hair and faces, then refreshing themselves with cokes and moving to the rubbing table where Doc Masters was working efficiently on one player after another. Shoot! Spike is right! We gave it all we had; c'mon, gang, tomorrow's another day.

Still in his wet clothes, the manager moved along the benches. "Why, Tuck, don't sit there in those damp things like that. Get yourself a shower right away. What's that? How's that, Harry? Never mind . . . you can't help it. . . . I didn't get me a hit either and I went up there seven times tonight. Won't do any good to sit and think about it. Besides, your ball in the fifth was through for a clean one only it took a charity hop right into his glove. You can only hit 'em, you know, you can't direct where the ball goes."

"Yeah, but shoot! That one I offered at in the twelfth was a low, inside corner pitch. I shouldn't have hit at it."

"If it was a good-looking ball, O.K. You got nothing to worry about; you're hitting three-fourteen right now; that's better'n all right in any man's league. And, boy, you're really playing third base for me these days. Yes, sir! How many assists tonight? Seven? Eight? Say, is that good?

And the stop you made off Crawford in the sixth—honest, I thought that one would knock you over, it was hit so hard. You know, Harry, I believe you handle those hot liners better'n any third baseman in this circuit. Yes, I really do. Now get yourself a shower in there and forget this game."

One by one the men dressed. The room emptied. Then over in a corner Spike saw a doleful figure on a bench, sitting unclothed save for a towel around his waist.

"Bonesy!" The youngster looked up. "What's biting you?"

The kid turned to his locker. He picked up his shirt and, slipping it on, started buttoning it listlessly.

"See here! You ain't gonna let this one game upset you, are you?"

"Shoot, Spike . . . seems like I'll never be a pitcher . . . never . . ."

"Stop talking that way, Bones. You're a pitcher now, and a darn good one. Ten hits in seventeen innings; that's pitching in any man's league."

"Yeah, and whad' I get out of it?"

"O.K. But you can't win 'em all, y'know."

"Aw . . . I chucked it away myself. I was so sure I had that man, that last hitter. . . ."

"Nosir, you didn't chuck it away. You slipped and fell; that happens to us all. Point is if it came the first inning you'd never have thought of it. It came at a bad moment; that's tough; forget it. Won't do you any good sitting here thinking about it. Get yourself dressed, go grab some food, and forget this evening. You're gonna win me lots of games before you turn in your uniform next fall, I'm fixed on that. . . ."

Slowly the boy dressed and went out. The room was empty now save for Spike and his two coaches, Cassidy and Draper. The three left together. Outside the park Bill Hanson was just climbing into a taxi. They shouted and climbed in beside him, everyone talking simultaneously. The conversation was acid.

"Shoot! We can think up more ways to lose a ballgame."

"I'll say. From where I stood, I could swear that drive of Swanny's was fair by eight inches. Did you notice the way it bounced?"

"These Cards are sure poison for us. They got the luck and nothing else but when we play 'em."

"Yeah, they just can't seem to lose. A pitcher holds 'em to ten hits in seventeen innings, le's see . . . that's seven hits after the first . . .

that's seven hits in sixteen innings . . . that's about one every other inning; then what? We lose because the pitcher slips, fielding an easy bunt!"

"How many hits did we get, Charlie?"

"We only got eight, I think. Unless they call that one Jocko beat out a hit. Did they call that a hit?"

"Uhuh, the scorers out here are lousy on those. Shoot, why can't we get some breaks? They get all the breaks."

"Yeah, and they sure know what to do with 'em when they get 'em, too."

"You talk about breaks! Tuck told me he lost that ball of Stevens' out there in center in the seventeenth. Seems he couldn't quite reach it; the ball bounced off the tips of his glove and then fell behind the flagpole, and he couldn't find the darn thing. While he was looking, the batter goes into third. How's that for a break?"

"Yep, or that hit of Red's. It struck the rail of the stands and bounded right back into Frankel's glove. An inch higher and it would have been a homer, one inch. As it was, Red was lucky to make second. There's a real break for you."

The taxi rounded a corner on one wheel,

shaking them up, and the conversation died away. The cab became silent, each man bitter with the memory of some one inning, some one play when a fraction of an inch or a fraction of a second would have changed the outcome of the game. No one spoke. They were all punch-drunk with fatigue and soreness over losing that important contest.

Finally Hanson, trying hard to see the cheerful side, interjected a ray of hope. "Well, we lost the game; but all the boys up in the pressbox would talk about was Hathaway. You got yourself a pitcher, Spike; he can really fog 'em in."

"You're dead right there, boy," said Cassidy. "He's not a rear-back-and-blaze-'em-through kind like Raz Nugent or Tommy Hedges of the Tigers; but he's fast, and he has one of the best curves I ever looked at. All this talk about his fast ball. Shoot, for my money his curve is his pay pitch. I bet the Cards think so tonight."

They turned the corner and came up the driveway of the hotel. The taxi stopped. A doorman in white opened the door of the cab. Leaving Hanson to pay the bill as usual, they stepped inside. In the lobby a bunch of kids were standing around Bones Hathaway who was buying a newspaper at the stand. Some of them detached themselves and swarmed over toward Spike, extending pencils and autograph books.

"Please, mister; please, Mr. Russell. . . ."

"No . . . nope . . . not tonight, sonny . . . not now. You all ought to be in bed by this time, anyway. . . ."

He stepped into the elevator. Hathaway and Hanson were standing together, an island in a sea of clamoring kids.

8

They sat at the table in the crowded grill, Hanson eating and enjoying his meal, Bones not eating and not enjoying it. From time to time he sipped the beer at his side.

"Why, boy, you pitched a whale of a game, good enough to win ten ballgames. What's a pitcher gonna do with a team that only gives him eight hits in seventeen innings?"

"They sure weren't handing me many runs, were they?"

"I'll say. And a manager who goes seven times to bat and can't deliver once. . . ."

"Yeah. But Spike's a good guy."

Hanson lit a cigarette. His tone changed; it

became warmer instantly. "Oh, he's a good guy, a great fella, Spike is. I like him. Point is, in this-here game you must deliver, boy. Don't make any difference how swell a guy you are."

"If only I hadn't slipped in the seventeenth out there."

"Shouldn't have been any seventeenth if he could only hit in the clutches. He never could hit in the clutches."

"In the Polo Grounds . . ." said Bones tentatively, attacking his food at last. Hanson interrupted.

"That was luck. He was shot with luck that day. Besides, that short right field fence, why, a kid could poke one over there. What I always say is this—Spike's a darn good ballplayer, but good players don't always make good managers. I've been around quite some time in this League, and I can tell you I've seen more than one fine player ruined by asking too much of him. Have another beer, Bonesy?"

"I oughtn't to. I've had two already."

Hanson paid no attention. "Waiter! Two beers, two more beers, please."

"Two beers. Yessir, right away, sir."

"Now you take, f'rinstance, Karl Case. There's a guy who's been around, too; he knows all the answers, he can really hit. And Spike ups and trades him for this kid Baldwin. I'm not saying Case was easy to handle; point is, that's what being a manager is, see? An older man would have worked on Case so's he'd be of use to the club. Whereas Spike gives up on him. He gives up too easily."

"They all tell me Case was something. . . ."

"Sure. But that's a manager's job. Here! Waiter, you with those beers! Right here. Thanks. A cold glass of beer tastes good after sitting in that fireless cooker all night. Now that's the trouble with a young manager; he gives up too quickly on a man; he hasn't had the experience McCarthy or McKechnie has. Just so soon as a player slips or throws a bad game, the young fella is ready to give up on him. I've seen it happen time and again. . . ."

Bones drank his beer eagerly. "Is that right? Is that so? Is that the kind of a guy he is? I didn't know. . . ."

"You watch. Don't take my word; you wait and see. 'Course I'm not saying anything out loud, y'understand. I'm simply telling you, Bonesy, personal-like, 'cause I think you're a good kid. So's you can sort of watch your step."

"Yeah, I appreciate it. Thanks lots, Bill. I'm glad you wised me up."

"Say! There's Baldwin . . . isn't it? With that girl friend of his . . . and another dame . . . there in the doorway?"

"Why, sure! It's Jane Andrews. They come from the same town, somewhere down in Tennessee. . . ."

"Hey, Clyde!"

The trio looked round, searching for a table. Clyde heard his name; he saw them and waved across the room.

"Here, sit down, sit down here." Hanson beckoned to them and they came over, Baldwin introducing the secretary to his friends. "I must get along anyway. Yep, I have a report to make out and some work to do. The boys play ball, Miss Andrews, and they're all finished, but the secretary never finishes." He grabbed the check from the table and wrote his name and room number on it. "Good night, everyone. Good night, Bonesy, and good luck to you, kid."

In room 1016 Spike Russell lay listening to his brother's snores. Makes a difference if you're a manager or just another player. Makes a big difference if you're carrying the team or just another guy out there with eight others. Well, that's what being a manager is, I guess. Ho-hum. Ho-hum. I must grab me some sleep. I need sleep the worst way. Sleep, that's what I need. No good thinking about that game, that one's gone, that's over and done with.

He didn't think he was asleep, yet he must have been, because without remembering where he was he suddenly woke up. Through his half-sleepy condition it all came back to him. Directly in front was Bones. He saw the pitcher run in, scoop up the ball, and all at once his feet went out, he slipped and fell. With sinking heart Spike watched him throw low to Klein at the plate from a sitting position. By this time Spike was wide awake. A bad habit, this business of waking up in the middle of the night, and he had been doing it lots lately as the team rose in the League standing, as the race became tighter, and as his nerves became more tense.

He turned over. Then he turned back again. His brother stirred uneasily in the hot room; he was sleeping badly but at least he was asleep.

Guess I'll get up and take a shower; why, I'm wet all over just from lying here. A shower would cool me off, it would do me good. Shucks, we never should have lost that game today . . . yesterday . . . never should have lost. . . .

Someone was singing outside in the hall. The voice was young, loud, raucous. Another voice broke in, trying hard to quiet him. The voices came nearer.

"Pahden me, boss . . . is that the Chattanooga choo-choo . . . track 29 . . . you've plenty of time . . ."

Someone bumped heavily against the door and sheered off. His companion was hushing him, but the voice continued as loud as ever. "I got my fare . . . and something to spare . . ." It moved down the corridor.

Spike leaped from the bed. No move he ever made on the diamond was quicker. In two bounds he was at the door. His brother had slipped the lock, and for a few seconds that were endless he fumbled with it before it opened. The voice, now familiar, was at the end of the hall, getting fainter and fainter.

"She's gonna cry . . . until I tell her that I'll never roam . . . Chattanooga choo-choo . . . won't you take me back home."

The door finally opened. Two figures, one with his arm half around the other's waist, were turning the far corner at the end of the corridor.

Spike stepped out and started after them, then realized he had nothing on but the trousers of his pajamas. Turning, he saw a man and a woman coming toward him from the other end of the hall. He ducked back, closed the door, and stood thinking. Somewhere in the distance the sounds of singing died away. He went quickly into the bathroom, turned on the light, and looked at his watch to be sure of the time. Three-thirty.

He was back now and had the telephone.

"Give me Mr. Hathaway's room," he said quietly. "That's right . . . J. B." The delay was interminable while the operator finally got the right room number. Then Spike could hear the phone ringing. It rang and rang. Finally a voice answered.

"Hullo?"

"This you, Bones?"

"Naw. It's Baldwin."

"This is Spike Russell, Clyde. Is Bonesy there?"

A second of silence intervened before the other replied. "Why, yeah, he's here. He's asleep. Want him? What's the matter?"

Spike was stumped. Clyde might be telling the truth. If he was, to wake up a boy who had gone through that three hour grueling on the field would be wicked. He probably wasn't asleep, to be sure. But he just might be. A guy could make mistakes.

"Nope. I'll see him tomorrow. O.K." He put back the receiver slowly. This being a manager was really no fun at all.

9

They sat on the edge of the seat in Spike's drawing-room on the train. Their faces were worried and tight. So was that of the young manager. He sat by the window looking out and talking all the while as if he were addressing the scenery. Both the rookies were speaking together when he interrupted.

"Look here, I don't care. I don't care for all that. I don't care where it was or how it happened. I don't care who started it. I don't care if it was only beer. This is a ballclub, not a reform school, and a man has to look out for himself. Now, Bones, and you, too, Clyde, this is the last time. Get me, the last time."

"Yes, sir."

"Yes, Skipper."

"You both remember what I said the other day in that meeting, don't you?"

They both nodded solemnly.

"O.K. That was last week. And you forgot it. In less than one week you go out and get high. . . ."

Their tones were a mixture of denial and hurt feelings. "Oh, no, Spike."

"Why, looka, Skipper, we only had a few beers."

"How many times do I hafta tell you it makes no difference if you only smelt a beer if you come roaring down the hall at three in the morning? And I don't care which one of you it was; all I care about is winning that pennant. Anything that interferes with that is out. Now, Bones, whad' I say in meeting last week?"

"Skipper, you said you'd fine us fifty bucks the first time."

"O.K. I kept my word, didn't I?"

"Yes, Skipper."

"An' what else did I say, Clyde?"

"Why, Spike, you said you'd fine a man a hundred bucks the second time."

"I'm gonna keep my word on that, too, even if

it is hard on one of you. I don't care, I want you to learn this lesson right now. If you must learn it this way, that's tough. Both you boys'll be short a hundred bucks on your next salary check. Get me?"

He paused, waiting. They both nodded. He knew he had struck home, because if one of them hadn't been drinking the previous night, they would have protested with heat. As neither of them spoke, he continued. "Now, Bones, whad' I say about the third time?"

Bonesy's voice was hardly audible above the rumble of the swaying pullman. "You said there wouldn't be any third time," said the young pitcher, looking at the floor.

Spike turned toward them. "Remember who I told that to? To Raz Nugent, my best hurler. And I mean it, believe me. This goes for him and for both of you boys and everyone on this club. Even if it costs me the pennant. Get it?"

They nodded, seriously. "All right. See you don't forget it in the future, 'cause I really mean business. Now get out; go get your dinner."

They needed no encouragement to leave. They rose without a word, pushed back the folding door, and slipped into the thick-carpeted corridor. Bill Hanson was coming down toward them.

"Hi there, boys," he said genially.

Neither rookie paid any attention. They had something else on their minds. The secretary stood to one side, his mouth open, as they passed. He watched them roll down the corridor and disappear at the end. He shook his head and moved along to Spike's room, where he knocked at the door.

Spike came down to breakfast the next morning at the William Penn with the *Post-Gazette* under his arm. Usually he went into the coffee shop where the team ate, but after the scene on the train the night before he wanted to avoid them all, so he went into the main dining room. At the door he ran into Charlie Draper who was leaving.

"Hey, Spike! Good morning!" Notwithstanding a night on the train and an early morning rising at six-thirty, the little chap was cool and dapper in a thin summer suit. "Ya saw 'em, didn't ya?"

Spike nodded. He disliked recalling the scene.

"They were mighty quiet lads at dinner last night on the train, so I figgered you laid 'em out properly."

Spike nodded and went inside. There were things he could talk over with Cassidy and

Draper; other things he could discuss with Fat Stuff and the old timers; and some things like the trouble with Jocko Klein and the bench jockeys he couldn't even mention to his brother. This was one of them.

He sat down and ordered breakfast. That must be Bill Hanson over in the corner. Bill was anxious to know what happened; he had hinted as much last night on the train. Gosh, there's some folks on this club think they know more about what's going on than the manager. Bill's into everyone's affairs; probably reporting everything to Jack MacManus, the club president, in Brooklyn, too. Sometimes Spike wondered just how much Hanson was really for him, despite his bluff and agreeable manner. He buried himself in the sports pages. There was an Associated Press story from St. Louis about the team.

"Although the Brooks dropped three out of four here, their playing impressed everyone, including their rivals. Lots of people thought that the newest and youngest pilot in the business was slightly wacky when he sold Slugger Case to the Braves for $2500 and an unknown fly-chaser named Clyde Baldwin, recently up from the Texas League. But the inside on this is that the Slugger has slowed up lately. Nor has the heavy hitting outfielder been carrying his weight at the plate, either, at least so far this season. According to the writers traveling with the club, the whole team has changed. They say there's a new spirit visible, that the boys are really going all out for Spike. While he's a youngster in years, he's been around plenty, and knows most of the answers. He needs to know them to handle some of the temperamental men on his club."

Boy, you said something! You really said something that time!

"Spike's pitching staff is holding so far. This boy Hathaway lived up to everything said about him in his first appearance in Sportsman's Park. He's a real find, and if he lives up to his promise he might turn out to be the rookie of the year."

Someone passed by at the side, and a queer inner feeling caused Spike to look up. He glanced back again quickly at his paper. Bill Hanson was leaving the dining room.

"Besides being the youngest manager in either league, Spike Russell is also the world's greatest optimist. Asked by this reporter whether his club, which has been back in the rut most of the year, still had a chance at the pennant, he replied: 'A chance? Sure we got a chance.' If Spike ever gets thrown out of baseball, he can always get a job in radio on that one!

"Here's the youthful manager's last word. 'Our spirit? Great! The boys are hustling because they know if they don't they'll be trying it on somewhere else. There's nothing wrong with our attitude. Look round and see for yourself!' "

Holy smoke, thought Spike, I must stop this sort of thing. Why, I'm getting to be a pop-off guy. Old Grouchy was dead right; when you don't say anything you don't ever have to eat your own words. Yessir, he was dead right. Some sportswriter over in St. Loo the other day asked him how Dusty Miller was making out at first. "He can play first," says Grouchy. That's all. And see how I popped off; talked three minutes to that reporter and he blew it up into a column and a half. I sure must be more careful.

Meanwhile up in Room 2516 the secretary sat at a desk covered with letters, telegrams, papers, clippings, railroad tickets, and various other things. His briefcase on a chair was smothered in more papers. His opened satchel also contained club documents. Sitting before the desk, he picked up the telephone and continued working as he talked.

"Hey there, sweetheart . . . how 'bout that call I put in for Brooklyn. . . . Triangle 5-2500 . . . Hanson, W. H. . . . John J. MacManus . . . this is 2516 . . . do I hafta go into all that again? . . . O.K. . . . yep, I'll hang on."

With the telephone in a vise made by hunching his shoulder and pushing it against his ear, Bill with two hands free continued working. He sorted out papers, scribbled short notes on letters, tossed telegrams over to the chair where his briefcase reposed, arranged clippings in small piles.

Suddenly he dropped the pencil and his left hand grabbed the receiver. "Yeah . . . yeah . . . O.K., go ahead . . . hello . . . hello . . . Jack! That you, Jack? . . . This Bill." A silence followed while he listened with a growing frown on his face. What he was hearing he evidently did not like. Finally he broke in.

"Sure . . . sure . . . sure everyone knew we needed that game the worst way . . . sure it was tough to lose . . . why, he slipped, that's all . . . he just slipped and fell . . . yes, he is . . . yes, he is a good fielding pitcher . . . well, yes, I have a theory . . . only I kinda don't like . . . O.K., if you want my honest opinion, Jack, looks to me as if Spike disliked the boy . . .

well, he's been riding him pretty hard, and you know how a rookie is. I think the kid's maybe lost confidence." Again there was a long silence save for the punctuations caused by Hanson's assents. "Yeah . . . uhuh . . . yep . . . I will, yeah . . . I'll keep my eyes open . . . yeah, I'll report. . . . I getcha.

"What's that? What story? Oh . . . that! Yes, I saw it. Well, Jack, you know what these sportswriters are; they hafta fill up the papers, don't they? Why, no, I wouldn't go so far as to say the piece is wrong; the spirit on the club ain't bad . . . well, O.K., maybe it's better'n that. Certainly the boys are trying, they're trying hard . . . but he's kinda a hothead . . . he gets all steamed up and rides 'em hard. I know for a fact he gave Hathaway and Baldwin a lacing in his room on the train coming over from St. Loo last night. Threatened to suspend 'em both. What for? Why, just for getting loose over a couple of beers after that long night game. How do I know it was only a couple? Well, I happen to know because I was in the grill of the Coronado with 'em myself . . . no, not at another table, at their table. I saw what they were both drinking, I saw the whole thing.

That's how I know. Yep, I will . . . uhuh. . . . O.K., Jack, I will . . . yep . . . g'by."

He rang off. He pushed the chair back and stood up. He wiped his forehead. Then he walked across the room, returned, sat down at the desk again, and finally took up the telephone.

"Hey there, sweetheart, this is Bill Hanson in 2516. I want the *Post-Gazette*. That's right. And look, see if you can get me Bill Smith, the sports editor, and tell him Hanson, the secretary of the Dodgers, wants him, will ya, please?"

10

It was warm that afternoon in the sun at Forbes Field, terribly warm, and after batting and fielding practice the majority of the team trooped into the clubhouse to change wet shirts, rest a minute, and enjoy a coke sitting on the benches before their lockers. Near Spike a salesman was trying hard to sell the rookie, Baldwin, a fancy pair of sun glasses. One of the things that had most astonished Spike and Bob when they first came up into the majors was the number of people who hang around a team making money from the ballplayers. There were the merchants who made you a tailor-cut suit, the real silk hosiery people, the life insurance salesmen, the automobile salesmen, the man in each city who could get things for you cheaper than in any other town, no matter what it was you wanted. By this time the sun glass merchant was almost an old acquaintance.

"Now these green ones here, Mr. Baldwin, the ones you have in your right hand, they are specially ground. They're for general all-round use. We call them the every-day pair. Then these polaroid glasses are for an afternoon of blinding glare, when the sun's particularly strong. All the stars use 'em. And the yellow glasses are for a fielder, now, like picking a fly ball out of a blue sky. You know how 'tis, one miss and there you are, there goes your ball-game!"

The same line, the same tune, same words he used on all the rookies. Then Razzle's loud voice across the room broke into the salesman's chatter. Raz was taking off his shirt and putting on a dry one, entertaining an admiring audience the while.

". . . So Rats, he takes one bite, puts down the tools, and calls the waiter over. 'I ordered breaded veal cutlet. Is this-here breaded veal cutlet?' The waiter looked at the plate, then he looked at Rats. 'Can't you tell by the taste of it?'

he says. 'No, I can't,' says Rats. 'Well then, what difference does it make?' "

A burst of laughter greeted this. The team's looser than when we were in St. Loo, thought Spike. Thank goodness, that tight feeling has gone. They're really loose today; they'll play ball this afternoon, I know.

Then Rats' loud voice could be heard from his corner. "Yeah, an' I remember when Raz and me was breaking in on the Waterloo team of the Three-Eye League. One day he ordered apple pie. 'Yes, sir,' says the waitress. 'A la mode?' Raz, he thought it over. Then he cracks: 'Nope, never mind. Just put some ice cream on it!' "

Laughter again. The laughter sounded pleasant in the ears of the manager. Then the voice of the astonished rookie behind came to his ears. "Six bucks! Six bucks for a pair of sun glasses! Why, I usta get 'em at the Five and Ten!"

"Talk about eats!" Old Fat Stuff's voice was low, but when he spoke everyone on the club listened with respect. "Years ago, when I made my first trip as a rookie with the Giants, we came north doing our tour with the Yanks, and Babe Ruth was along, his last season. Boy, could he stow the food away! When he got through with a roast chicken, it looked like an old catcher's mask."

The boys started to go out. Razzle's voice could be heard long after its owner had disappeared. ". . . I was playing then with Hartford in the Eastern . . . boy by the name o' Wright . . . always had a wad of gum on the button of his cap, and if two strikes were called on him at the plate he'd take that wad off and chew it like hell. You'da died laughing the day we sprinkled it with red pepper . . . he jumped like somebody give him a double hotfoot."

Bob, almost the only player in the room, walked across to the rubbing table, hidden by a curtain at the side, for a last minute rubdown by Doc Masters. Stealing second the previous day he had strained a muscle in his leg. He let down the trousers of his monkey suit, took off his sliding pads, and showed the sore spot to the Doc who felt it gently.

"Ya got about ten minutes, Doc, just a few minutes. If you'd give this the once-over, please." The Doc leaned over and looked at it intently, his practiced fingers diagnosing the trouble immediately. Bob climbed up on the table and the Doc started gingerly to work. Soon the place was empty, save for Chiselbeak, the locker-room man, moving around and straightening things out after the players. He was talking to someone.

"Yeah, them lads is good. They're both good. If they don't make it with this bunch, they'll make it somewhere else."

"They'd make it here all right if they were handled properly." From behind the curtain Bob recognized the voice of Hanson, the club secretary.

"They've been trained right. You'll hear how important a big league manager is; what I always say, it's a manager in the minors who's important."

Boy, you're certainly correct, thought Bob, only half paying attention as he relaxed under the comfortable glow of the infra-red lamp on his sore muscles. Chisel, you've got something there; you really know your baseball. Then Hanson's tone or his words suddenly made him pay attention closely.

"You said it, Chiselbeak. If they don't get their fundamentals in baseball down there, they don't ever get 'em up here. Why, anyone ought to be able to manage those two kids. This Baldwin can hit. He's a free swinger, have you noticed? He holds his bat loose and away from his chest. And Hathaway's a real pitcher. I see where a guy in the paper this morning calls him the rookie of the year."

"I seen that. Wouldn't surprise me none, an' I been around plenty."

"You and me both, Chisel. We been with this club a long while. Now you take me. I've been on the inside of major league ball for almost fifteen years. So what? So that hothead Jack MacManus goes haywire and makes this kid manager who's only been three seasons or less in the majors."

"Well, Bill, you know how Jack is. . . ."

"Yeah, he goes off half-cocked more often than not. Well, you and me, Chisel, we're old timers round here. Then this kid, this johnny-come-lately gets to be made manager. That's how things are. 'Course I'm only talking to you, Chisel, y'unnerstand."

"Oh, sure, I getcha, Bill."

"Well, I'd better get out there. He's gotta win this one today; he's on the spot this afternoon. He'd better win this one."

Hanson's voice died away and his footsteps sounded outside the room. Chisel continued hanging up clothes, opening and shutting lockers.

Bob sat up. "Thanks, Doc. That feels much better. I'm glad I slipped in and let ya work on it, mighty glad."

11

Spike lay there yawning, his hands behind his head. The room was hot even at eight-thirty in the morning, betokening another steaming afternoon at Forbes Field. In the other bed Bob snorted and turned over. That boy, he can sleep all day and all night. Give him a chance and he'd just never wake up at all. It's different when you're running the team; when you're the manager and responsible for things; when you've got everything on your neck. You wake up then fast enough. You wake up in the middle of the night and you can't get back to sleep for thinking of this and that; or you wake up before daylight and lie there wondering who to pitch that day, or why you didn't pull off the hit-and-run in an important moment the afternoon before. You go all over the things you must do, and think of all your problems. You got plenty of 'em, for you have twenty-four ballplayers and every single man is a problem and a new one. You get rid of one problem; you imagine you're all set, and then bang! Up comes a different problem. A pitcher like this boy Hathaway who's temperamental. Wouldn't you think these kids would realize what a chance they have and tend to business!

Well, that's how things are; one problem after another. When you get up there in second or third, when nerves become tighter as the season gets longer, the problems multiply. Still and all, we've done pretty well, if we lick these birds today, we'll go home tied for second. That's all right; that's as good as could be expected; that's better than all right when you consider we were in sixth place when I took hold in July. Why, we could even beat those Redbirds. I mean, we gotta chance.

His brother stirred. Spike realized he had been muttering out loud. He jumped out of bed and went into the bathroom to shave. I must be going nuts, he thought, talking to myself like that!

That afternoon, in their last game on the western trip, the team threw away a golden chance. The Cubs were leading the Cards, and the Dodgers, watching the scoreboard, started to press. They wanted to win too badly. They made errors. Rog Stinson had one of the bad days that come to even the most experienced hurlers; a day when nothing went right, when he hadn't a thing on the ball. In the second the Pirates scored three runs, filled the bases, and knocked him from the box. Spike was obliged to call on Elmer McCaffrey, who was lucky to put out the fire. This upset the pitching schedule, because he had counted on using McCaffrey in the doubleheader against the Giants the next afternoon in New York.

McCaffrey was in one serious difficulty after another, but partly through his own skill, partly because of the fine defense of the Dodger infield he sneaked out of every hole. Yet the team looked bad. In the seventh the Pirates loaded the bases again and got two more runs. The Cubs had scored four runs off a Card pitcher and knocked him from the box, so neither team seemed likely to lose ground to the leaders that afternoon.

Now then, thought Spike as they came in to the

dugout, it's the ninth and we're five runs behind. But I'm not giving up yet, no siree; I'm not giving up. By golly, I'll never give up on this club; nothing is impossible with this gang. Nothing.

"Uncross those bats, boy, uncross those bats there." The noise ran up and down the bench; Razzle's bark and Bob's shrill-voiced pepper and Swanny's deep-throated roar and Roy Tucker's chatter.

"C'mon, gang, le's get us some runs. Five runs! We've done it before, we can do it again."

Jocko Klein, the first batter, hit a slow, bounding roller to the left of the pitcher and tore for first.

"Hurry, Jock! Get the lead outa yer pants! Hustle, kid . . . looka him go. . . ."

He was safe. The Pirates protested but he was safe. McCaffrey was at bat, and the veteran pitcher was a good hitter. He waited for a full count, and then a shout rose from the bench as the man in the box lost him. It was evident the Dodgers weren't the only ones to feel the coming of September in their tired bones.

"Whitehouse, number 18, running for McCaffrey." Swanny next forced Klein at third on a bunt that was too deep. Shucks! One out and men still at first and second. Now then, Red, old kid, you can do it. Pick us up; you've picked us up more than once in a pinch like this. We sure need a hit; get us a hit and keep us going.

The veteran first baseman waited for the full count and then leaned into one and drove it hard to right center. He was perched on second and two runs were over when the ball got back to the infield.

Here's Tuck! Roy Tucker came to the plate, the crowd yelling. Spike watched him as he touched all four corners of the platter for luck. One out, a man on second, and the enemy bullpen swinging furiously into action. You could never tell when the Dodgers were beaten; this might be a ballgame after all.

Roy swung off his heels and missed. The next pitch was low, inside. The hands of the umpire went to the left.

"Ball one."

Then another ball. Then the center fielder laid down a perfect bunt, in the ideal spot halfway between the plate and third. The pitcher raced over, so did the third baseman, who charged in, got to the ball first, and threw.

If they catch that boy they'll hustle, thought

Spike. If they nip him they'll move fast; Roy's a speed merchant . . . safe! He's safe!

An angry crowd of Pittsburgh players surrounded the umpire at first. The man on the sack, furious, hurled the ball into the ground before his feet. Suddenly a piercing shout rose from the diamond and from the bleachers behind third. The first baseman jumped down, grabbed the ball, whirled and burned it to the plate. Big Red Allen, on second, had started with the bunt, rounded third without pausing, and roared home. His two hundred pounds straining to give everything he had, legs extended, arms up, he came charging into the plate in a smoke screen of dust as the ball reached the catcher above. The umpire, bending over, extended his hands. Another run across.

When the noise subsided, or as it was subsiding, Roy Tucker was sliding head first into second. The catcher, off balance, threw quickly and the ball got past the shortstop into left field. Roy picked himself up and came into third standing. Meanwhile at the plate Red Allen rose slowly from the dirt. Spike ran over and helped the big chap to his feet, walking back to the bench, his arm around him. "Red, by golly, before I came to this club I always thought you were the greatest first baseman in the game. Now, doggone, I'm sure of it!"

The veteran leaned over, shook the dirt from his uniform, and grinned. "We'll get 'em for you yet, Spike."

Gosh, what a team! They're money players; looks like they've got to be spotted a couple of runs before they really bear down. What a team they are in a pinch!

"All right, gang, le's go! Here comes another pitcher, boys; here comes a new man. What say we get this one? O.K., Clyde, one man down and a runner on third." Nervously swinging two bats, Spike Russell stood in the circle watching his star rookie in the batter's box. Holy smoke; he's cooler'n I am. But we sure need this game. If we can only grab off two more runs and take second place tonight, we won't ever look back; I know we won't.

Baldwin hit cleanly into the hole between second and first. Tucker came across with the fourth run. What a crowd to play with! They're just never beaten. Now it's up to me.

The man in the box was keeping the ball low and outside, Spike's one weakness, but at two and two he hit. A weak one, in the air. He ran hard to first but the yells from the stands told the story. He was out.

Shaking his head, he returned to the dugout. Shucks, that's not backing them up like I should. I ought to have crowned that second pitch, that fast ball. You can't hit if you don't take your bat off your shoulder. And my timing is way off these days. But we aren't licked yet; Harry Street always picks me up.

Harry caught the two and two count and laced the ball over third down the left field line, a good clean single. Baldwin was coming into third, and Spike, tense and anxious, stood on the step of the dugout watching Harry race like mad, head down, for second base. The throw was to third, it was wild . . . c'mon, Clyde, c'mon in. . . . Holy Smoke, now Harry's going into third! What a ballplayer that guy is!

Baldwin was in and Harry slid safely into third. The bases were cleared ahead of him and the score was a tie at five apiece. When Bob swaggered to the plate, Spike hardly dared look, feeling certain his brother would bring home the winning run. He did. His shot bounced against the scoreboard; 475 feet from home plate.

Now the Dodgers were leading; they were ahead by two runs, but they weren't yet out of the woods. For in the last of the ninth the Pirates came roaring back, angered at seeing a game already won snatched from them. The first batter hit a sizzling bounder through the box. Spike darted across. It was a hard ball tagged for center field, yet he had stopped harder ones. So he went all out, racing desperately over to stab it back of second. Then, in his hurry, he made a mistake. Off balance, he threw to Red.

The throw was so wild not even Red could block it, and the runner, without pausing, rounded the inside of the bag and started for second. Then Spike saw Jocko Klein. He ran to back up first on every ball hit to the infield and one never thought about it, never even saw him. Now, when he was needed, you suddenly saw him and your heart jumped. Because that error could mean the ballgame.

The stocky catcher stopped the ball and then, without hesitating, burned it to second. Spike, waiting, slapped it on the runner just as he came tearing in, and the man was out. One out, instead of a man on second with no one down. Well, that's picking me up; that's certainly picking me up all right.

Then Speed Boy Davis, the pitcher who had gone in for McCaffrey, weakened and lost the next batter. Once again there was a runner threatening. Gosh, won't this ever end? Is this going on all night? Spike retreated to his position, glancing back at Rats Doyle throwing in the bullpen, watching Speed Boy carefully. He's tired all right; he's really tired. If this man gets on I better yank him.

They all expected the man to bunt. That was percentage baseball. He did. The bunt was well placed, between the pitcher and first, and Davis went over. It was a slow hit, and he was near first when he scooped it up. He straightened as he got the ball, and threw it over Red's head into right field. Immediately the runner on second broke for third, and the batter roared into second despite Swanny's recovery and quick throw. The winning run was at the plate.

Davis was weakening in the heat and the long, exhausting game. When he passed the next man to fill the bases, Spike turned and waved to the bullpen. As usual Rats, warming up, pretended not to notice him. They stood around the rubber, Spike and Bob and Harry and Red and Davis, gloomy and silent, saying nothing because there was nothing to say, while the crowd in the stands began shrieking for a hit to win the game.

Shoot! That's awful bad. Davis knows better

than to straighten up on a play of that kind. He was just plain tired; he didn't stoop down, he stood up straight and let go. Shucks! You practice and practice and practice a play all spring; then comes an important moment in a vital game and someone forgets everything he's been taught. That can cost us second place.

Now old Stubblebeard, the umpire in charge, was becoming impatient. He went out to deep short and waved for Rats to come in to the box. The big lefthander swaggered across the field, accompanied by hoots and claps from the bleachers. Spike kicked at the dirt in the pitcher's box. This is going to raise hob with my pitching schedules. This will upset everything. Now I don't know who'll pitch tomorrow. Shoot, I don't know who'll pitch the next inning, if there is any, and it certainly looks as if there would be now. But we need this game the worst way; we simply gotta have this one.

The Pirate coach held up one finger to the baserunners. Three men on, one out and two runs behind. Rats pitched. The batter hit the first one hard, to Spike's right, the sure test of a shortstop. It was a ground-hugging hopper, and the Pirate baserunner hid it momentarily, then jumped it and was off toward third as the bounder sizzled toward Spike.

Now . . . careful . . . steady . . . make it sure . . . don't throw before you have it. . . .

He sent the ball away cleanly and fast to his brother on second. Bob jumped deftly out of the path of the spikes of the Pittsburgh runner charging into second, and got the ball off quickly to Red on first. One out! Two out! Almost before the batter had slowed up back of first they were running in, stuffing their gloves in their pockets, racing toward the showers. As they roared past the dugout, Chiselbeak was already lugging out the bat trunk and throwing the bats into it. Within the clubhouse the equipment boxes were set out before each man's locker. These small, oblong wooden boxes had a space at one end for caps, and a large place for wet clothes, the whole to fit into the equipment trunks. It was the usual sign that meant a change of scenery. The western trip was over and the Dodgers were headed for home in second place.

12

The American rocked along the rails through the gathering dusk. The players had eaten and returned to their air-conditioned rooms. Red Allen, quietest and most reliable member of the team, was deep as usual in a crossword puzzle. Razzle, neither the quietest nor yet the most reliable member, had dropped in and was sitting with his feet on the opposite seat.

"We sure needed that one. Boy, we needed that one. And we could use those two against the Giants tomorrow. There's a couple of good ballgames to win. Second place ain't bad; it ain't bad, kid." Then he added: "That is, if we stay there!"

"We'll stay there," replied the big first baseman not glancing up from his crossword puzzle.

"Yeah. Looks like this-here club is moving the right way at last. Say—d'ja hear about those fans who started that fight by calling Jocko Klein names over in Phillie in June? Remember? Their case came up finally. The judge fined them twenty bucks and sent 'em to the cooler for ten days."

"That right. . . ."

"Uhuh. Fine and cooler, eh!" The first baseman was too deep in his crossword puzzle to get it.

"Razzle, what's an eight letter word for satisfy?" The pitcher reflected a minute. "Highball. At least there's a few guys on this club what seem to think so. Hey there . . . hey there, Jocko! Boy, you really backed us up out there today; you were really on your toes, Jocko."

The black-haired catcher passed by in the corridor and paused, smiling. "Anyone hear how those Redbirds made out this afternoon?" No one knew, so he moved along.

In the next compartment, Rats Doyle was talking to young Hathaway. "Say, are my dogs tired! That gettin' up and settin' down and gettin' up all afternoon tires a man more'n pitching a full nine innings of ball."

"Being a relief pitcher is no joke," said the rookie, sympathetically.

"Boy, you oughta have been on this club last season under Nippy Crane. It was something. A guy was in and out, in and out, every other day. I was a regular pinch pitcher; in more games than a playground director. So was Fat Stuff. He was in the bullpen so much he got his mail there."

"It's different now."

"I'll say," agreed the relief hurler, kicking his shoes off and pushing them to one side. "Are my dogs tired! Yep, Spike Russell stays with you to the limit. He used more pitchers today than any time for a long while; he likes to give a man a chance to win his own game. Over the long haul it teaches you to rely on yourself, not on bullpen support. I b'lieve it helps a manager, too. Look how some of these boys have come along in the past few weeks. Why . . . hullo there, Swanny!"

The big, blond fielder rolled past. He entered and slumped down. "Well, here we are, going home in second place. Darn it all, who'd have thought such a thing could happen? Who'd have thought it possible two months ago?"

"You said it, Swanny. Looked to me like we were anchored in sixth place."

"For life, if you asked me."

"Yep, and since then we've won . . . what? 48 out of 62, isn't it? 48 games out of 62 since Spike took over. How's that? .700 baseball, isn't it?"

"Yes, that couldn't be just a coincidence. Say, I sure hope we don't run into another convention in New York when we get there. Everywhere we run into conventions; in Pitt it's a druggist convention, in St. Loo an undertakers' convention, in Chicago an Elks' convention; seems like a man can't get a decent night's rest any more!"

In the compartment at the end of the car, Spike Russell, alone, was reading the morning New York newspaper, just arrived by air. He liked to keep track of what the writers, traveling with the club, felt and what they thought about things.

"If the Dodgers win today, they'll go into second place, and if they do it's speed more than anything which yanked them up there. They aren't the Dodgers any more; they're the Swifties. They get a man on first, you look at your watch to see the time of day, you glance back, and the guy's sliding into third. How he got there is a mystery; hitch-hiking a plane most likely. The miracle is the way their manager, young Spike Russell, shook this team up, bought a player or two, made a few trades, got them playing together, injected speed until at present it's the fastest club in baseball. And so into second place."

There was a knock at the door. He set the newspaper down. "Come in."

The door opened and in came Doc Masters, the trainer, wearing a worried look on his face. He closed the door behind him and stood there. Now what?

"Sit down, Doc, sit down. What's up?" Spike knew it was bad news. When anyone came to see him, it was always bad news. When things went smoothly, they let him alone.

"Spike, I hate like hell to cloud up and rain on you right now, but this kid Hathaway . . ."

"What's he done?" Spike sat up quickly.

"Why, the crazy young fool, you know how superstitious these boys are; well, seems he had herring and bacon and eggs for breakfast the morning of the day he pitched that game against the Cubs. Then he goes in and holds them to a couple of hits. So he's eaten the same breakfast eleven days straight now. Naturally, it caught up with him. He's got a bad case of indigestion, and if you ask me, it's a wonder he hasn't come down with ptomaine or something worse."

"Confound these kids! Don't they ever think? How long will he be out?"

"Why, Spike, that's kinda hard to tell. You certainly won't be able to use him against the Giants; thing of this kind is weakening. You might throw him in against the Braves at home the last of the week; I won't promise though."

"Shoot! I was counting on using him in turn. Well, that's baseball for you."

The Doc shook his head. He had a long knowledge of the game and its personnel. "That's baseball players, you mean." He left, and soon after Charlie Draper entered. The coach was in a rare good humor. His reddened countenance beamed from the effects of a good meal and a cigar. The day's work also pleased him.

"G'd evening, boss. That was a swell one to cop off this afternoon."

"Yeah, it was, only . . ."

"These boys are beginning to be a team now. Lemme tell you, too, that lad Baldwin can really hit. He makes me think of Cobb and Ruth and the best of 'em. Don't fool yourself, he's a natural hitter."

"Yes, he's sure gonna be useful this year."

"Spike, I been watching him at the plate. They've curved him, they've pulled the string on him, they've hi-lowed him, they've thrown him everything but the kitchen sink, and still they can't seem to get him out in the pinches. I asked him to account for it at dinner."

"Thasso? What'd he say?"

"Says, 'I guess it just happens that the pitchers out there are throwing where I'm swinging!' "

"Well, I wish they threw that way to me. I've gone one for seventeen this week. I can't seem to buy me a base hit these days."

"Spike, know what I think? You're pulling your fanny away from those inside pitches. You aren't hitting like you used to hit; you're hitting like old Case did toward the end, with one foot free."

"I'm not conscious of it."

"You are, just the same. I was watching you carefully this afternoon. You gotta stay in there, gotta keep that old right foot solid. Now that's what I like about this kid Baldwin, his stance."

"It ain't his stance that worries me. It's his roommate. You know what that crazy kid has gone and done?"

"Who . . . Baldwin . . . Hathaway?"

"Yeah. Ate herring and bacon and eggs for breakfast eleven days running; now he's laid up with a bellyache and can't pitch at the Polo Grounds tomorrow."

"Shoot! We wanted his game the worst way."

"Of course we did. I'm not sure if Hathaway is the man for Baldwin to room with. Two young rookies like that living together may be bad. I'm thinking of breaking 'em up and putting Hathaway with old Fat Stuff Foster."

"With Foster? Don't do it, Spike."

"Why not?"

" 'Cause it won't work out. The kid wants to live different from the old man. Fat Stuff he wants to live different from the kid. And these pitchers are so darn temperamental, you put one of 'em in with a guy they don't happen to know very well and they may go all to pieces on you just when you need 'em bad. I've seen it happen."

"Yes, and I've seen it happen the other way round. I've seen a young rookie cooled off living with an old timer."

"Maybe. Sometimes it works out, I know. Well, you're the manager, Spike."

That's it. He was the manager. And here again

was one time when being manager was no fun at all. He thought about it at breakfast before the train pulled into the Pennsylvania Station. They were slightly late when they finally did stop and the team piled off. Spike, with Bob at his side, went up an escalator, followed by the rest of the boys.

As they reached the top a strange sight met their eyes. Although it was still early in the morning, a vast sea of people, a huge semicircle of curious faces dotted at intervals by policemen, met their astonished gaze. Then there was a shout, a dozen shouts, a roar.

"Hey there! Spike . . ."

"Where is he . . . where is he. . . ."

"An' Bob . . . an' Raz Nugent. . . ."

The shrieks and cries burst into a roar. They were in the midst of a sea of fans. They fought their way up a flight of stairs and there a still larger crowd greeted them. The noise echoed against the lofty vaults of the station, it increased with the appearance of every new player, it grew louder, louder. Suddenly the crowd broke the police lines and Spike was seized from behind. His feet went from under him; his bag was snatched from his hand. He was above everybody, looking down on them from someone's shoulder, looking on an ocean of excited, upturned faces; near him Razzle was also tossing on an angry sea, and even big Swanny was coming up to join them, and others. Then the cops began clearing a narrow passage through the mob, and the Greenpoint band began blaring somewhere up ahead, and they were being rushed across the station floor to the open-mouthed astonishment of the few early morning patrons of the road. While all around and behind rose that roar.

Well, that's baseball for you. That's being a baseball manager.

Baseball nothing! That's Brooklyn.

13

"Whitehouse, number 18, batting for Hathaway, number 15." The loudspeaker droned the words above the shouts and yells of the fans.

It's the suddenness of baseball that makes it such a game. A team goes rolling along with everything clicking, the pitcher throwing shutout ball, the fielders making brilliant stops and grabbing liners off the fences, the opposing batters retreating inning after inning to the dugout in disgust. Then with no warning the storm breaks. The club that is moving like a machine falls apart for no reason at all.

That afternoon, with Bones Hathaway pitching

brilliantly, the club had a comfortable lead of two runs going into the seventh against the Boston Braves. Not a man had reached second base, and with two down in the first of the seventh Hathaway seemed to have a no-hitter in his grasp. Then the strain told; the effects of the long season began to show, and he weakened. A base on balls was followed by the first clean Boston hit of the game, a stinging drive over second base. The next batter dumped a short one in front of the plate, and Jocko Klein, who was usually death on those balls, fumbled it momentarily. The bases were filled.

A two-bagger down the line, a lucky drive that missed first by inches, cleared them. Then the Boston catcher caught one of Bones' fast balls and drove it over the fence. A game that had seemed to be in the bag suddenly went out from under. The score was five to two.

At last they came in shaking their heads. Shoot! Do we always have to win the hard way? Do we always have to come from behind? Can't we ever have a day to coast home? That was the hardest part of it, the feeling once more of having to pull up from behind, the necessity once more for giving from their store of nervous energy, of drawing again on those hidden reserves which they had been using so frequently of late. Yet something inside each man forced him on when his whole being told him he couldn't; something inside every man refused to let him quit. They had to struggle on.

So they stomped into the dugout, hot, wretched, perspiring, angry, nervous, upset. "Five to two. We gotta do it; doggone, we gotta do it, that's all. Seems like we always hafta win the hard way." It wasn't any doubt of their ability to pull it off in the clutch that bothered them; it was a doubt as to whether once again they would be able to call on that painfully small reserve of nervous energy which was left.

Bob, the first batter, responded by singling to center, making Spike tingle all over. What a ballplayer, yep, and what a brother he is! Always there when you need him; what more can a guy ask? Now, Jocko-boy. Jocko Klein shuffled up to the plate. After trying twice to bunt and fouling off each time, he struck out.

Spike looked down the bench.

"O.K. . . . go up there, Alan; go up and take a cut at that ball."

The loudspeaker droned its message. "Whitehouse, number 18, batting for Hathaway, number 15."

The boy responded by hitting a stinger to the left of second base; but the shortstop nabbed the ball and Bob was lucky not to be doubled, saving himself only by a fierce scramble back to the bag. Swanny, the next batter, tried hard; but his deep fly was caught close to the fence, and there they were going into the eighth, three big runs to the bad.

The Braves went down quickly before Rats Doyle, the Brooks' relief hurler; but so did the Dodgers in the last of the eighth. Then the top of the ninth and the last of the ninth, with the score still five to two. As they came running in for their final raps, a quick shout went up around the stands. They turned back and saw a figure 6 in the fourth inning of the Cards' game against the Phils in St. Louis. It was all right to say don't watch the scoreboard. But those six runs for the St. Louis team didn't make pleasant reading. It tightened the tension inside the Brooklyn dugout.

"Three runs. Only three runs, gang. We can do it against these palookas. That guy in there is a big fellow; he's tiring; he's plenty tired right now. Only three runs, gang; le's go get 'em. We can do it!"

Of course they could. They believed this, they

knew they could. Hadn't they been coming from behind to win all season? Wasn't that their specialty? They could do it if only they could summon those reserves, if only they could call on that extra bit of energy and will power and determination, which they had been so recklessly spending all summer. Now they were down to the bottom of the barrel and their reserves were dangerously low.

Harry Street stood at the plate cautiously waiting for a good one to hit, fouling off pitch after pitch, until the weariness of the man in the box was visible by the length of time he took to get ready, and the way he stood with hands on hips beside the mound, panting.

Three and two. Three and two, what'll he do?

He clouted it, a fierce liner over second base. Then the shortstop appeared from nowhere, flying through the air to spear the ball, falling in a heap to the ground. He rolled over and over but came up with it in his hands.

"Can you beat that? A drive that wouldn't be stopped once in a thousand times. Shucks, honest, howsat for bad luck? Just when we need hits like diamonds." The bench, which had jumped up with the sound of the bat, subsided in agonizing silence. To lose that one hurt. Harry Street returned, shaking his head.

"Hard luck on that, Harry!"

"Boy, that's tough; that's really tough, Harry."

"O.K., Bobby, save us one up there."

From the bench Spike watched the familiar figure of his brother at the plate, thinking of the many long hits the boy had made throughout the season. Just get on, Bob, he said to himself; get on anyhow, anyway at all.

Bob got on the right way by smacking a solid liner into left field that nobody was near, took his turn, retreated to first, stood there and exchanged his batter's cap with Johnny Cassidy, the coach. Spike spoke to Fat Stuff at his side on the bench.

"Freddy, y'know I b'lieve that man is really tiring, that pitcher. He's tired; if we can only get a man over now. . . ."

Jocko Klein, at the plate, waited carefully. The Braves' hurler threw wide on the first pitch; but the catcher refused to go fishing. He fouled off a low one, then another. Then another. Yet somehow his swing lacked conviction; there was no authority in it. Finally he worked the count to three and two.

The next pitch was low and Klein trotted down

toward first. Spike watched him go carefully, noticing that there was no spring in his step. These boys are just plain tired, that's all. They're tired, they're feeling the long summer, the pull-up, the strain of this campaign. Why not?

Now the stands were up, waiting to see who would hit for the pitcher.

"McCaffrey, number 19, batting for Doyle, number 6." Spike was desperate now, trying every possible method of working in those runs. Elmer McCaffrey, besides being a good relief pitcher, was an excellent batter himself. But he wasn't equal to it that afternoon. A long fly was hauled down in center field, and neither runner could advance.

Then Swanny came up to the plate, nervously touching his cap, swinging his club, doing all those things a man does unconsciously in a tight spot. The pitcher was annoyed. He, too, was weary and nervous, but couldn't betray his feelings. He waited until Swanny got through fiddling round, then he called time and stooped down over his shoelace.

Swanny immediately backed away from the batter's box, as the crowd jeered him. Then he stepped in. The Braves' hurler took the rubber;

but the little duel was not over. Swanson, in his turn, called time, stepped back again and knocked the dirt from his spikes. And ever and always that fearful figure 6 on the scoreboard beside the word St. Louis looked bigger and bigger. Two out, and three runs to the bad.

At last everyone was ready. The catcher gave the sign, the man in the box nodded, checked the men on base, and wound up quickly. He pulled a string and it was right over for a called strike. The next pitch was a strike, too.

From the dugout, Spike heard his brother's cocky call. "The big one left, Swanny old kid, the big one left."

That's what it was, the big one. Swanny met it, hard, and from the sound everyone knew the shot was deep. The left fielder, running desperately, charged headlong for the stands. He looked up just in time to save himself from crashing into them. The ball was disappearing in a mass of frenzied kids in the stands above.

The dugout dissolved in a fever of joy. Jackets and caps and towels went into the air and fell outside on the well-worn ground. Someone upset the bat rack; the bats tumbled out; behind them the fans went wild. Pandemonium conquered the park, while the three players trotted around the bases. Half of the Dodger team was at the plate to meet them, and Spike, throwing his arms around big Swanny, hugged him as he charged over. Across the way, the Braves' dugout was the only quiet portion of the field.

Now the score was tied, the Brooks were back in the ballgame. A new pitcher shuffled across. From the dugout Spike saw Townsend, the Boston manager, shifting the outfield as Clyde Baldwin, his young slugger, came to bat. Townsend moved the score card in his hand to the left, then he rose, stood up, and holding it horizontally in his hand moved it again. Meanwhile the pitcher was standing in the box, and Baldwin was waving his bat threateningly at the plate. After a few moments of signaling and wigwagging, everyone was set. The man on the rubber took his sign from the catcher and threw. He only threw one ball.

Clyde Baldwin caught it squarely and hoisted it high, deep, over the right field fence. Up, up, up and down. It disappeared into Bedford Avenue. Before he reached the plate the crowd was pouring onto the field below, and most of the Dodgers, to avoid the mob, were racing for the showers.

The clubhouse was a happy scene. Spike came

in, proud of his team, watching them peel off wet clothes, yelling at each other, their fatigue forgotten. No one had to urge them that afternoon to get their clothes off and get into the showers; they were ready enough that day. Only Jocko Klein sat quietly on his bench, weary and beaten.

Doc Masters, the trainer, came into the manager's dressing room as Spike, without any clothes on, stood talking to Charlie Draper, the bat bag in his hand as usual.

"Spike . . . this kid Klein . . . he has what it takes."

"You tellin' me! He's a bear for work. Charlie, know what I think about that boy? He's a short kid, only five feet eight or so. I think a feller that size has to be extra good to make a team. Understand what I mean?"

The Doc interrupted. "I'm telling you he has what it takes. He caught that game today with five degrees of fever!"

First Hathaway, then Klein! Just with the critical series against the western teams coming up, too.

Spike's first thought was for the club. "Is he . . . will he . . . is it serious?"

"Nope, it's just a touch of intestinal flu. That

hot weather in Pitt and those darn air-conditioned rooms and trains, they raise hell with a man when he's tired. Like Klein is. The wonder to me is we haven't got more of it. He'll be O.K. in a couple of days—say by Saturday. But with five degrees of fever—why, most guys would have been in bed this afternoon."

Spike threw a towel over one shoulder and went out to talk to the catcher, followed by his trainer.

Yeah, and most guys wouldn't have made this team, either.

14

The Braves left and the Phils came to town. The Phils departed, and the Giants moved over from the Polo Grounds. The western clubs next descended upon them as the days shortened, and the heat of summer gave way to cooler days and longer nights. Braves, Phils, Giants, Reds; it was all the same to the Brooks. They assaulted each team in turn, running up their string of victories to five, to six, to seven. They had been ten games behind the worried Cards when they started in August, five games early in September, then four games, three games, and at last two games. And as they came roaring up the stretch, tense and tight and tired and lame, it wasn't the Dodgers who looked like cracking when the crisis came.

Their rise was easy to explain. They were a unit, a team playing together. They had this spirit and something more; they had five hitters in the three hundred class; they had the one-two punchers in the National League in Roy Tucker and the freshman, Clyde Baldwin, walking up his heels; they had a wise and knowledgeable pitching staff, strengthened by young Hathaway who was developing into the rookie of the year; they had an infield as solid as a rock; a veteran at first base, who knew the answers and was always there in the pinches; a snappy young second sacker who was a holler guy, the spark plug of the team on offense and defense; a shortstop, who was a manager plus, who could go far to his right and make the hard plays look easy; and a reliable third baseman, with a wonderful pair of hands, who kept the hot corner under control, coming up with stabs and stops at vital moments in tight games to turn hits into doubleplays. Add to all that the fastest outfield in the business, and there's a prescription for a winning club.

When they came up within a couple of games of the League leaders, Spike, ever the same, began to feel worried himself. That afternoon Bones Hathaway became a whitewash artist by throwing his tenth shut-out of the year, and the team clinched second place. That evening Spike called together his general staff; the coaches; Doc Masters, who knew every man's physical condition; and Fat Stuff, the old hurler who was as much coach himself as player. They had sixteen games left, and their handling necessitated the help and background of men older and wiser than himself.

In his suite in the hotel he began talking about the thing close to his heart; this club, his club, his men and their chances.

"They're tired, these boys, believe me they're plenty tired."

"So are you, Spike."

"No more'n the rest of 'em."

"Well." Old Fat Stuff puffed on a stogie. "Well, these boys have been pulling themselves up by their bootstraps since the twenty-third of July. You gotta have what it takes to do what these kids have done. Why sure, it leaves you gasping for breath. Then, too, the strain reacts on 'em physically, I think. . . ."

Doc Masters spoke up: "Yes, the boys are getting tight, an' I find in baseball, when players get tight . . . when they get tight they always get injured. There's hardly a one hasn't got strawberries or slide burns or a lame back or something. Roy Tucker ran into the wall the other day and got banged up real bad, and Harry Street isn't over that beaning yet; he ought not to be playing. Now the pitchers . . ."

"We're no worse off'n the Cards. I see where Rackenbusch was knocked out in Boston the other day. Just tired, he is."

"Yeah, but you take our pitchers, they all have sore arms or legs 'cept Hathaway. Take Rats Doyle, f'rinstance; there's a big guy, a worker, a rubber arm; he gets the ball over; he knows what it's all about. Well, he's been in as a relief . . . three . . . four games since . . . in the last ten days. He's tired. D'ja notice Raz Nugent toward the end yesterday?"

"Did I notice him!" Charlie Draper spoke up. "In the sixth, when they tied it up there, I asked Raz when we came into the bench how he felt. 'The old pusher's kinda tired,' he says. 'An' look at my bunion, Charlie.' Know what? He takes off his shoe and stocking right out there on that bench."

Spike laughed. "Say, I bet I looked at Razzle's bunion one hundred times this season. Always looks the same to me. He's that kind of a pitcher; if he gets a lead and keeps ahead, his bunion never bothers him. But when they began to hit him there in the sixth yesterday, he suddenly thinks about it and his bunion started to hurt. That's baseball for you."

"Shoot, the big cry-baby!"

"No, you're wrong there," said the Doc. "He's not a baby; he's a pitcher. They're all that way. Razzle's a good guy; he'll pitch his old heart out if you ask him. But when he thinks he's slipping, when he gets tired and loses control, he gets worried."

"Yeah, know what? When I see Raz out there on Friday, I walked to the bullpen to ask Rog Stinson, who's warming up, how he feels." Spike shook his head. "He says he feels fine. Next inning, when they get to Raz, I shove him in. They score three runs and like to cost us the game. Afterward in the clubhouse, I find out from Kenny, the bullpen catcher, that Rog told him just before I come up, that his throwing arm was sore as all get-out."

"Then why didn't he say so?"

"Didn't want to quit, that's all. Didn't want to pass the buck to Rats Doyle."

"Boy, that's tough."

"Nope, it's baseball. It's part of being a manager. This is a dead game bunch of guys. . . ."

"You bet they are. Any team that can do what this gang has done isn't finished until the end. How many more do we play now?"

"Sixteen. Thank heaven, we're in our own back yard until the finish."

"Spike, you know what? It looks to me the way the club is rolling, those games against the Cards might decide the pennant."

"Most likely they will. We're only two games out now, if we hold on like this . . . " He paused. A voice penetrated the smoke-filled room. It came from the corridor outside, a young, lusty, and confident voice.

"She's gonna cry . . . until I tell her that I'll never roam . . . Chattanooga choo-choo . . . won't you. . . ."

"Won't you take me back home." Two voices went down the hall, roaring at the top of their lungs.

"There's two boys is loose and easy," said someone. The room listened. Then the singing died away as the pair turned the corner at the far end of the corridor. Spike looked at his watch; eight-thirty. Hathaway, feeling high after his shut-out that afternoon, and Baldwin, doubtless, equally so after a triple and a homer against the Reds' best pitcher, were together. They'd bear watching, those kids. Maybe they were all right; maybe they'd take in a movie and come back to bed. Maybe not. He made a mental note to check on them later in the evening.

But it was a long while before the Dodger board of strategy broke up, for there were many things to settle, and when Spike found himself alone he was worn out. Forgetting his rookies and their troubles, he climbed into bed. His brother tiptoed in, undressed in the bathroom in order not to disturb him, fell into bed, and almost immediately began to snore. Not Spike. He tried to sleep, but the harder he tried the more wide awake he became. He wasn't worrying about the club, but he had to think about something and the club was on his mind. Hours went past. Darkness finally gave way to dimness; dimness to dawn; dawn to daylight.

Someone was knocking, knocking hard and with insistence. He woke from deep slumber, certain he hadn't slept at all. It was broad daylight; Bob heard the noise and stirred uneasily. The knocking continued. Hang it, a telegram most likely. Spike sat up in bed, rubbed his eyes, sleepy and annoyed.

"Yeah. Who is it?"

"It's me. Swanny."

Spike jumped from the bed. Swanny, one of the most reliable members of the team, must be in trouble. An accident, an injury, trouble of some sort and serious trouble. Bob, now awake and startled, too, sat up blinking as Spike rushed to open the door.

He opened it for Swanny. For Roy Tucker and Rats Doyle also, all of them dressed. They said nothing but pushed past him into the room. He looked at his watch. It was exactly seven-thirty.

He closed the door, closed it on someone and quickly opened it again at another knock. Freddy Foster, followed by Red Allen, entered. Then McCaffrey and Jocko Klein and Raz Nugent, a scowl on his face. Spike stood sleepily in his pajamas, rubbing his eyes as they filed in. They sat on chairs, on the bed, stood by the windows.

"What the . . . what's biting you guys?"

No one spoke. There was a queer look on several faces.

"What's biting you, calling a meeting this hour?" said Raz.

"A meeting! I never called a meeting. What is this?" Now he was furious, angry at having been called from a sound sleep.

They all started talking at once. The telephone operator had called every room, told them to report at Spike's suite for a meeting at seven-thirty.

Spike grabbed the phone, irate, weary, sore. The door was still opening for the latecomers. He got the assistant manager. That gentleman went to another phone and talked to the operator who had put in the calls. The night before she had received orders to call everyone at six-thirty for a seven-thirty meeting.

Spike put down the phone. He was plenty mad. But he couldn't be mad with the boys; nor they with him. Plainly, someone had played them all for suckers. "Wait a minute . . . who's missing . . . anyone missing?"

By now the room was full of sleepy, irate, and breakfastless ballplayers, angry at the trick that had been played. Who's missing? Everyone looked at everyone else.

"Whitehouse?"

"Here I am!"

"Elmer McCaffrey ain't here."

"Hell I ain't!"

"Harry Street. Street, Harry Street."

Then the door opened and Harry walked in.

"Hathaway!" exclaimed someone.

"Hathaway!"

"That's right. Hathaway."

"Hathaway . . . and Baldwin."

"Let's get them guys!"

"Let's go for 'em!"

"What's the room number? Get the room number, Raz."

"You'll do nothing of the sort." Spike took command. "You guys go down to breakfast, and let me 'tend to this. Now get out. And leave those boys alone, hear me?"

They turned to leave, as disgruntled a bunch of ballplayers as you could find. But they knew their manager. When Spike got his dander up, he could be plenty tough. They decided to leave things to him.

15

Evening. Spike sat waiting for his young rookies to come to the room. He sat in the easy chair with the lamp behind it, newspapers on the floor at his side, another one in his hand. He was reading Tommy Heeney's column in the *Mail*, and for just a minute he forgot the problem before him.

There was a knock at the door.

"Come in."

They entered, two worried boys. Spike tossed the newspaper to one side. He got up and closed the door.

"Sit down, Bonesy; sit down, Clyde. I wanna have a serious talk with you two. Guess you know what it's all about." Now comes the tough part. Grouchy would handle these birds right. But now it's up to me.

"Boys, lemme ask you something. If you were out there in a tight game, and either of you came up to the plate with the bases full, you wouldn't strike out each time on purpose, would you?"

"Why, no, of course not."

"You wouldn't try to make it harder for the boys than necessary, would you?"

No, they wouldn't. But they were puzzled. It was plain they were puzzled. Spike went on, not so sure of himself.

"That's what you did when you woke up twenty-two men this morning."

They spoke together. "Spike, we didn't do that."

"Now, looka here, boys; let's get this one straight. I happen to know you were out last night."

"No, sir. . . ."

"No, we weren't, Skipper." Their tones were firm. "We only went to a movie, then we stopped in for a couple of cokes, and we were both in bed by eleven."

"Bones, I'm not going to ask what you did last

night or where you went. All I'm interested in now is that someone pulled a schoolboy trick on us. They gave orders to attend a meeting in my room here, and woke the boys up at half-past six."

"Spike, we had nothing to do with it."

He looked at them both. They both looked back at him. And they seemed to be telling the truth. He was perplexed

"Boys, I'd like to tell you something." He decided to take another line. "This race is tight. I feel it, same as you and everyone. You boys can loosen up once in a while; I'm the manager, I can't. An' I don't sleep so good, either. Last night I saw dawn come. That's a fact, I never got to sleep until daylight. Then just as I'm dead to the world, the boys start knocking the door apart."

"Gee, Skipper, that's really tough."

"Yeah, well, whoever did it has me sunk. Now you boys both have the goods. But you've both been hard to handle ever since you came on this club and . . ."

"But, Spike, we didn't have a thing to do with this; we didn't know about it till we came down to breakfast."

"O.K. O.K., if you say so. Just the same,

you've both given me trouble before. Bones, you made a fool of yourself eating that breakfast of herring and bacon and eggs ten days . . . eleven times straight. Well, that's a typical rookie trick. You were lost to the team for almost a week; and I overlooked that. But we're coming up to the pay-off now. I wanted to break you and Baldwin up several weeks ago, and I was advised not to. Wish I hadn't taken that advice. I know how 'tis, a man gets used to another roomie and it upsets him to change, especially if he has only had one roommate since he came to the club. But I've got to go through with this. Tomorrow you'll move into Freddy Foster's room, Bones."

"Me? Room with old Fat Stuff?"

"That's right. And Baldwin will go in with Harry Street. They're older men, they're married. They like their rest every night and they'll make darn sure they get it. See you get yours, too."

"All right, Spike, if you say so."

"Remember, one more flare-up and you go off to some other team, and take it from me, no manager wants boys on the club that's likely to cause trouble, no matter how good they are.

"So this is your last chance. Stay with us,

boys. See here, you two have everything. I don't ask much, all I want is you should keep in good condition for these next vital games we're running into. Do that, and you can pretty near name your own figures on a contract for next season. I don't usually make predictions, but here in this room I'll say that if you stay in condition, you boys, we'll grab off the pennant. Now that isn't asking too much, is it?"

"No. No, Skipper, it isn't."

"Nope, it isn't, Spike."

"All right. Go get yourself a good sleep tonight, and tomorrow pack your stuff and move into your new quarters. And mind you, remember what I've been saying."

He held out his hand. They took it. Their faces were sober. "O.K."

"O.K., Skipper." The door closed behind them as they went out.

16

Now it was ding-dong, hammer and tongs, everyone all out every minute of play in those tense, torrid days of September as the team crept steadily up, their hot breath fanning the red necks of the nervous Cards. Four games back the first week of the month, then three, then two as the teams came down the stretch in the final fortnight of the season. You picked up the morning paper and figured percentages until you knew them by heart. Fifteen games to go, four games behind; twelve games left, three games behind; ten games to play, and two games back.

And every inning, every pitch and every throw

worth a thousand dollars. No wonder the stands were packed each afternoon, no wonder long lines stood waiting for tickets, no wonder the team was pestered by sportswriters who once had believed the young manager to be a bit on the soft side. They had never imagined the Dodgers could come from sixth place at the end of July, with the season more than half gone, up to second.

Now things were so tight it was necessary to go into fractions to figure out the standing of the two leading teams of the League. With the Dodgers having an extra game to play, this is how they stood.

	Won	Lost	Pct.	Games to Play
St. Louis.	98	49	.688	3
Brooklyn.	97	49	.685	4

Four games for the Dodgers, one against the fifth place Cubs, and then the vital three against the Cards. So a victory that afternoon would put them in a tie against the leaders, leaving everything depending on those last final contests.

The sportswriters stood around Spike before practice that steaming September afternoon as he sat on the spare rubbing table, thumping his glove with his fist, long legs dangling, trying to answer the questions from the group among whom were many strange faces. Lots of people had suddenly discovered the Dodgers were news.

"The Series? Oh, yes, the Series." He answered vaguely. "Well, I'm not worrying about the Series. All I'm thinking about is one game at a time. We're going out for this one; to hell with the Series."

They wanted more, they became inquisitive, they peppered him with queries. "Well . . . for one thing, I treat my players the way I want to be treated. The way Grouchy Devine always handled us in Nashville. I never call a man down before the others. I don't believe in tearing a clubhouse to pieces after a defeat. There are no second guesses and no post-mortems. I try to encourage initiative. Once the game starts, I leave the fellas pretty much on their own. Give boys a chance to play their game, and they'll carry the load for you. One thing I do insist; I make an effort to impress on them that today's game is the important one. . . . How's that? What say, Stanley? They call us what? They call us lucky?"

He laughed, a pleasant, agreeable laugh, yet there was tension underneath. "Maybe so.

What's wrong about being lucky? They can't put you in jail for that." Everyone joined in the general laughter.

"You got 'em fighting hard, Spike," rejoined the sportswriter.

"Stanley, when the going is good it isn't tough to fight hard. Anyone can manage a winning club. But when you're down in the second division, then it's no fun to keep struggling. That's what my boys have done. They hustled and they fought when things were blackest. They took up the slack of a poor start, they felt we ought to be somewhere up there at the end of the season, and we are. We take baseball seriously because it's the most serious thing we do."

He looked challengingly from one man to another; from the strange faces to the familiar ones; from the old timers who traveled with the club and were friends, to the columnists in search of a story for the next day who were strangers. Somewhere in the rear a voice murmured something about "the old college try." It was hardly a complimentary tone, and Spike instantly accepted the challenge.

"Yep, that's correct. This team has the college spirit; that's the way we came up. There isn't a single man on my club who considers himself a star. That's why we play well together, why we've been able to come from so far back to fight for the lead."

Then came the old question. "The pennant? Well, we try not to play the scoreboard; we try never to worry about the other man. I'll say this, though; as for the pennant, well, I think we gotta chance."

Laughter. Afterward the query he had been dreading because it was the one for which he had no answer.

"What about yourself, Spike? At the dish you haven't been connecting lately. How do you account for your slump?"

"I don't really know. Maybe I've been striding too soon; that's the cause of about 90% of all batting slumps in my opinion."

"Has being manager made any difference? Too much responsibility running the team?"

"Nope, that really doesn't bother me out there. It's just one of those things, I guess. You all know what ballplayers say: God takes you up to the plate, but he leaves you on your own when you get there." He slipped down from the table, disengaging himself from the circle. This was too personal. Hang it, whenever Grouchy held a press conference and someone asked a question he didn't want to answer, he always had one stock reply. "Suppose you let me worry about that." If Grouchy had been caught on the ark with Noah he would have said, "Looks like rain." Nothing more.

That afternoon they were not yet facing Grouchy, but playing the Cubs to win that extra game and so even things up for the final series. Spike started Rats Doyle and kept Razzle and Bones throwing in the bullpen, ready to jump in at the least sign of danger. He wanted to save his two star pitchers for Grouchy and the Cards, and his strategy worked. Rats was superb. He began confidently, went from good to better, and after passing the third batter to face him in the first inning, not a man got on base until the sixth when he lost another Cub hitter. Both were defeated trying to steal by Jocko Klein's iron arm.

The crowd yelled louder and louder with every out. The pitcher sat chewing vigorously on the bench between innings, trying hard to pretend it was just another game, not a crucial contest. Beside him the players leaned on every ball that was hit.

Following that long series of hard-fought, extra-inning games, this was a relief after the first Dodgers came to bat. The Cub hurler was throwing a grapefruit with seams, and the Brooks teed off on him. In the third they put over five runs. Then with the score mounting in the sixth to seven runs, and to nine the next inning, Spike began yanking some of his tired veterans. Whitehouse took over right from Swanny, and Roth came in at first for Red Allen, and in the eighth Raz, who had been in the bullpen, received the signal to come in and take his shower. Pausing for a minute to watch his teammates go to work on the third Cub pitcher, he stood on the step of the dugout, drinking a cup of water.

"I wonder they wouldn't take out that pitcher; he hasn't not done nothing yet," he remarked.

"Say! That's something even for old Raz. A triple negative."

"Aw." The big pitcher turned toward the bench behind. "Think I don't know the King's English, hey!"

"Razzle knows the King's English all right; trouble is, he doesn't care if he is."

Laughter ran up and down the long seat. They came into the ninth with the score still nine to nothing, three putouts from victory, from a chance to tangle on even terms with the Cards for the first time.

Rats Doyle never pitched as carefully as to those three men. One after the other, each man walked to the plate in tension. The first fouled to Roth behind the bag. The next man hit a mighty clout to deep center. Roy Tucker was going back, Roy the ever-dependable. He ran, turned, and stood there. He thumped his glove with his bare fist as he waited nervously for the ball to descend, that reassuring gesture which meant he had it. Down it came, he swallowed it, and the roar could have been heard in Boston.

Now one more out. The last batter was forever at the plate. He waited, he fouled off pitch after pitch, he ran the count up; one and one, one and two, two and two, three and two. He fouled off another, he slashed a hard drive down the left field line which was outside the base by an inch. Then he hit the ball in the air.

Thirty thousand mouths opened, thirty thousand throats bellowed, thirty thousand fanatics jumped up and down as the ball hovered in the air, high, back of the plate. And the dark-haired catcher threw away his mask and darted for it.

"Now, Jocko, now, Jocko . . . all yours, Jocko-boy . . . grab that ball, kid . . . grab that one and they'll give you Brooklyn Bridge. . . ."

He watched it in mid-air. He came back slowly, following the path of the ball as it descended. His mitt was close to his body, chest high, the open part up. His stocky legs were braced now. The ball came down, plunked into the glove. And stayed there.

He turned, held it for a second in the air so everyone in the feverish crowd could see, then stuffing it into his pocket he wheeled and rushed for the dugout.

Now then, bring on those Cards.

17

The clock on the wall above the bar showed almost eleven o'clock as Bill Hanson lit a cigarette, swallowed the last of his drink, and strolled out into the lobby toward the elevator. He got off at the twelfth floor where the club always lived; but instead of going to his own room he turned the other way, moved down the corridor and knocked hard on one door.

"Come in." Hanson turned the handle and entered. Bones Hathaway in his shirtsleeves was all alone. He sat in the easy chair under the lamp, relaxed, reading the sports pages.

"Hey, there, Bonesy. Where's Fat Stuff?"

"He had to go home tonight. Seems like his

missis is taken worse. You know she's been sick. Don't that beat all, the night before we . . ."

Hanson paid no attention.

"Fat Stuff! Fat Stuff! Why, he's so old he creaks. It ain't Fat Stuff that's worrying me. It's Clyde Baldwin."

The lanky boy in the armchair sat up. He and Baldwin had come up the hard way beside each other and a tie existed between them. If Clyde was in trouble, he, too, was affected. "Clyde? What's up?"

"He ain't in his room, that's what's up."

"How d'you know?"

"I just been there to give him his tickets. Here's yours." He held out an envelope. The young pitcher took the envelope and tossed it on the bureau.

"Say! That's bad."

"I'll say. After what Spike told 'em about turning in early tonight. If he finds it out, that kid'll be through. On this club, anyhow."

"Now where d'you suppose . . . whad' you think . . . he didn't say anything to me. . . ."

"I'm not sure, but I'll tell you what I think. Remember that dame, that girl from his home town?"

"You mean Jane Andrews?"

"That's the one. The babe he was in the Coronado grill in St. Loo with that night."

"Yeah, that's her. They come from the same town somewhere in Tennessee."

"Uhuh. Well, seems she opens at the Kit Kat Klub tonight. Y'know, Bonesy, it wouldn't surprise me a bit if he sneaked off to see her show."

"Why, he wouldn't be such a fool . . . he wouldn't."

"But he liked her, didn't he?"

"I'll say! He's nuts about her. Wait a minute." He stood up, yanked the newspaper from the floor. "Yes, sir. Yes, sir, you're right. Bill, you're dead right. She opens tonight."

"Say, if Spike Russell ever finds this out, that boy's goose is cooked. He won't play baseball on this club again, that's a cinch."

"You said it. I wonder if we could . . . that is someone could . . . what time is it?"

"Eleven-fifteen. I certainly wish it wasn't the night before this game. I'd grab a taxi and get that kid back in his room before anyone knew he was missing. But I got four hours of work ahead of me before I can hit the hay."

Bones was grabbing his coat from the bed. "Leave this to me."

"What you gonna do? Be careful, Bonesy,

you're kinda taking a chance yourself, beating it like this."

"Nuts to that! I'm not going to see Clyde Baldwin ruin his season and throw a World Series cut out the window for that dame, not without a try, anyhow. He's too darn good a pal."

He shoved his purse in his pocket. He was out the door. "No, sir, I'm not letting that girl ruin Clyde's whole season; no, sir, I'm not." And he was off. Hanson trailed after him.

"Now be careful, Bonesy, be careful. If anyone sees you coming in late . . . remember now. . . ." But Bones was down the hall ringing for the elevator.

Just at this moment Spike Russell in the other corridor came into his room, shut the door, and taking off his coat emptied the contents of his pockets on the bureau. His purse. A lot of miscellaneous junk. Some cards, one marked "Jack Schwartz, 50 Prospect Avenue, Brooklyn." Jack, besides being an undertaker, was also the Number One rooter of the Dodgers, sometimes even accompanying the club on their western trips. There was an envelope with tickets for a game several days before which he had forgotten to leave at the box office. And a small, creased paper. He opened it. In his own handwriting was a list of pitchers for the month of September, with the number of days' rest each would have. It was torn and dingy, having been in and out of his pocket dozens of times in the past month. All past history, now.

He next emptied the pockets of his trousers, took out his keys, his change, a handkerchief, and stood there looking almost fondly at that list before him, absorbed in it, in what it represented, thinking of those struggles, of games won, pulled out in the last innings, yanked from defeat when hope was gone, when most teams would have given up.

The door slammed. His brother came in and stood there looking at him.

"What's cooking?"

"Whad' you mean?"

"You were talking just now as I came in."

Talking! I must ha' been talking to myself. I must be going nuts. I'm talking out loud to myself and don't even know it. Holy smoke, this being a manager is getting me down.

His brother came over to where he stood beside the bureau and put his arm on his shoulder. "Take it easy, old timer. We'll pull this out for you."

"Thanks, Bobbie. You betcha. Thanks."

There was a knock on the door. Bob went over and opened it to disclose Bill Hanson. The burly secretary came in genially smiling. If he felt the pressure the club was under as they came into those final games, he didn't show it. With a smile he flipped two envelopes from his pocket.

"Here y' are, Spike. And here's yours, Bob. You wanted three, didn't you?"

"Three. That's right."

"Believe me, I had trouble laying my hands on 'em. Everyone in this club is on my neck, and we could fill the Yankee Stadium six times over for these games." He walked across and picked up the telephone. "Twelve sixty-one. That's right. Harry, this Hanson . . . is Clyde there? Clyde; Hanson. Yeah. I got your tickets. O.K., see me in the morning at breakfast, will you? O.K." He rang off. Then he picked the phone up once more. "Twelve sixty-nine." There was no reply. "Oh, sure, must be someone there. You aren't ringing the right number."

Spike, hanging his coat in the closet, looked up. "Twelve sixty-nine . . . who's that, Bill?"

"Hathaway. Seems funny. His room doesn't answer."

"Doesn't answer at all? Where is he? Where's Fat Stuff?"

"Fat Stuff's wife is sick. He went home to spend the night with her. Nope, there's no one there. I had a couple of seats for Hathaway."

"Give 'em to me. I'll see he gets 'em." Spike spoke with grimness. Both the other men in the room knew that Hathaway was in for a calling-down.

"O.K. You take 'em off my hands, will you, please? I'll be obliged." There was a cheery note in his voice as he handed the envelope to the young manager. "He's dropped down for a coke, mos' probably. Looks like this heat's gonna hang on all winter, don't it? Well, so long. Turn in, you guys, and get your rest now." He shut the door and was gone.

Spike looked at Bob and Bob looked at Spike, both thinking the same thing. It isn't possible! It just isn't possible that kid is on the loose again, after all that's happened. Surely he wouldn't go wild the night before this game. If he has, thought Spike, he'll get the worst going-over he ever got in his life.

The young manager went over to the telephone and tried to get the boy's room. It still gave no answer. Ten minutes later he stalked down the hall, knocked hard on the door; no answer again. He returned, fumed, looked at his watch.

Eleven-forty. At midnight he called once more without result and then asked for the desk.

"Leave a note for Hathaway in twelve sixty-nine, please. Ask him to report in Spike Russell's room at eight-thirty tomorrow morning."

He reached over, turned out the light, and lay down. But not to sleep.

18

An ounce of curiosity plus a pound of brass coupled with the sensitivity of a rhino and the pertinacity of a tiger; that's what makes a reporter. A few of the things, anyhow. How do they work, these mysterious fellows? How is it they invariably manage to smell out trouble on a ballclub; how do they always know when something important is about to break, someone to be traded by the club or sent back to the farm? In a word, how do they do their job?

In a dozen ways and none of them the same. Every reporter is an individual with methods of his own that work for him alone. One man is simply lucky. He's the sort who always seems to be on the spot when things happen, when someone calls someone else an ugly name in the dressing room, when a notorious character strays off the reservation at night, when a star loses heavily at poker in a closed compartment on a limited train. The reporter's colleague, who seldom has luck, is intimate with one of the veterans on the team who knows everything about everybody. A third reporter is a shrewd guesser, with a feminine sense of perception; he keeps his ears flapping, hears bits of conversation, asks questions. Questions like this: Say, what's wrong with Joe? What has Tommy gone and done now? Is it true that Bill is in dutch with the Skipper?

It was sheer luck that Jim Casey of the *News* happened to meet Bill Hanson in the lobby the next morning, and seeing the big secretary at the cigar stand, his usual bunch of newspapers folded under his arm, went over. But Bill was not his genial self, and instantly Casey was warned. He could detect small things like changes in mood; that was why Casey was a good reporter. He began to query Bill vaguely. Trouble? Oh, no, nothing. Nothing at all. Everything's fine. Just a rumor, that's all; nothing definite, y' understand, just a rumor; only . . . well . . .

somebody said someone was seen at the Kit Kat Klub last night. If so, it's too bad for him, that's all. Spike Russell isn't the guy to stand any fooling.

This was all Casey needed. He waited not a second, but went into the telephone booth and called Spike's room, glancing at his watch. The time was eight-thirty-eight. The young manager was there and awake, too, judging by his tone which was unusually crisp and sharp. Was any member of the team at the Kit Kat Klub last night and, if so, who was it?

Spike hesitated a minute. What's that? He asked Casey to repeat the question. Then again there was a silence. He replied noncommittally and rang off.

This was sufficient for Casey. And Stan King of the *Telegram*, who happened to be passing just as he emerged from the telephone booth with the look on his face Stanley knew so well, knew that meant something was popping. So he, too, went for Spike. In ten minutes it was all over the hotel.

At nine-thirty Bob, unconscious of the spread of the disaster, came out of the grill and went upstairs. As he came down the hall toward his room, he heard the telephone jangling inside.

He opened the door. The phone had been ringing for some time, and when he reached it the voice on the other end was angry.

"Spike! What in the hell ails you, anyhow?"

"This ain't Spike, Mr. MacManus, it's Bob."

"Oh! Bob! Where's that crazy brother of yours?"

The voice was determined. What on earth has Spike done now? "Why, I dunno, Mr. MacManus. I guess he's downstairs, or maybe he might be in Charlie Draper's room."

"Have him call me. Right away. What's biting him, firing his best pitcher. . . ."

"Firing? Firing who?"

"Bones Hathaway. He suspended him for the rest of the season."

Bob was stunned. Spike's a hothead; Spike's gone and done it again. Yet he couldn't somehow believe it. "But I . . . but he . . . but Bonesy. . . ." When Bob had left the room to go down to breakfast, Spike was merely going to give him the once-over, to let him have a call-down. Now he returned to find Bonesy fired. "How do you know? Why, that ain't possible; we need Bonesy out there this afternoon. . . ."

"How do I know? I know because Hanson just

phoned me. It only happened an hour ago and. . . ."

Suddenly words echoed in Bob's head. They were words he had heard long ago, words he had heard with dislike and uneasiness, words half-forgotten in the heat and excitement of the campaign, which somehow had stuck with him. He heard them once again, distinctly. They were the words of the big secretary. Not in his usual genial and agreeable tone; but whining words that were unpleasant to hear as he talked to old Chiselbeak, the locker-room man, in the cavernous clubhouse on Forbes Field.

". . . You and me . . . we been round this club quite some time, Chisel. Now, me, I've been fifteen years in the big leagues . . . then this johnny-come-lately . . . this . . ."

MacManus was ringing off. "Yes, sir. Yes, sir, I'll tell him," said Bob, half-dazed as he put the phone back.

". . . This johnny-come-lately, this . . ." The words echoed and re-echoed and bounced crazily in his head. He couldn't make sense out of it, yet he had the feeling that there was something wrong somewhere. Somehow some of the pieces didn't fit. There's a whole lot of things screwy and I'm gonna make it my business to find out what's what.

Bones Hathaway in twelve sixty-nine was in the act of jamming down the lid of his second suitcase. He was in his traveling clothes, the costume he always wore when they were on the road, a pair of fawn-colored slacks, a silk sports shirt open at the neck, and a sports coat. He was tanned, brown, sinewy, healthy-looking. There was a worried look on his face, however, and his greeting was abrupt.

"Bonesy! What in the hell's cooking here?"

The pitcher straightened up. He was tall and his shoulders were broad above the long body. "I'm through. Catching the noon plane home."

"But what . . . what's happened? For Pete's sake, what's up?"

"Spike! He fired me. I'm washed up."

"Hey, looka here! Tell me now, what's this all about? Spike's a reasonable guy; he was plenty mad at you last night 'cause he was tired; but he'd got over it this morning. When I went down to breakfast he was waiting just to give you a lacing, that's all."

"Uhuh. I was out until twelve-fifteen, see!"

"I know, I know, sure I know that."

"An' someone called Spike while we was

talking this morning, and told him I was at the Kit Kat last night."

"But you weren't, were you?"

"Yeah. I was."

"You were? Oh, that's bad; that makes things different; that's a different story, that is."

"Only I wasn't up there chasing a dame. I was chasing Clyde Baldwin."

"Baldwin?"

"Sure. It seems he went up to see that skirt of his. She was opening last night. I tried to nab him and bring him back. I was scared he'd get caught out. But the crowd was so darned big I couldn't find him. An' it was twelve-fifteen when I got back. Then this morning some guy phones Spike and tells him . . ."

"But look . . . but listen . . . why didn't you tell Spike? . . ."

"I started to. I didn't want to give Clyde away. I told him I had a special reason for going up. He wouldn't listen. He didn't care. . . ."

"But . . . but . . . yeah, but, Bonesy. . . ."

"So." He shut the second suitcase. "I'm through. Good luck, kid. You're a swell little guy, and you've got the best pair of hands I ever had behind me at second base. I'll be seeing you. And I'll be pulling for you, alla time."

"Here! Wait a minute! Hold on a sec. How d'you know Baldwin was up there? D'ja see him this morning?"

"Nope. But I know he was. Hanson told me so last night. He caught him—or at least he wasn't in his room about eleven when Bill went to give him his tickets."

Hanson. Hanson again. Hanson who griped to Chisel in Pittsburgh, Hanson who spoke to Hathaway the night before, Hanson who telephoned MacManus, Hanson who . . . this began to . . . began to shape up . . . to look all of a piece.

The telephone rang. "Yeah. O.K. O.K., I'm all packed. I'll be right down." He put back the receiver. "It's the bus for my plane at La Guardia. Leaves in ten minutes. G'by, boy. We had us one swell time together, didn't we, kid?"

"Now listen, Bonesy, wait a minute. Wait a sec, will ya, please? I'm mixed up on this; but yet and all, it don't somehow piece together. Wait a while; don't be in such a rush, Bonesy . . . wait a minute, please, will ya?"

But the big chap grabbed his two suitcases and threw open the door. The star pitcher of the Dodgers was leaving for home on the morning of the most important game of the season.

19

A large green car swung boldly in ahead of Spike's taxi, and the driver turned into the parking space opposite the field. Four attendants rushed together to open the door. It was Razzle's pale green Chrysler Imperial, with the maestro himself at the wheel. Others besides Spike Russell recognized the great man, and an army of kids dashed across the street, risking death under the manager's taxi, to demand the pitcher's autograph. Razzle finally squeezed his two hundred pounds from under the wheel, backed away from the car, and carelessly handed one of the attendants a half dollar tip. He strode over to the entrance, a massive island surrounded by an agitated ocean of beseeching youngsters.

Spike followed. In spite of the anguish in his heart, he couldn't help smiling at Raz's confident manner. The team might be in the critical contest of the year, everyone could be tense and tight; but Razzle was as loose as ever. To him it was just another day's work. While they dressed silently, the flow of chatter continued without pause from his locker.

". . . Time we was together on the Seals . . . one day I says to him, I says . . . 'Bill,' I says, 'Bill, this is your chance today. This is where you get that offer from the big time. No foolin', there's a couple of scouts here today; they wanna see you right after the game. Said they'd be waiting back of third base.' Well, sir, Bill plays his old head off, collars four hits outa five times at bat, and really turns it on in the field. When it was over, he couldn't wait to dress; he rushes over back of third base and, sure enough, there they were, too. A coupla 12-year-old Boy Scouts, asking for his autograph. Say, was he burned up!"

Razzle roared at his own joke. But the rest of the team dressed in silence. They sat serious and solemn-faced, oiling their gloves, getting ready for the conflict ahead with heavy hearts. A few leaned over, discussing the situation in half-tones, shrugging their shoulders when asked questions by the reporters, of whom there were plenty on hand. The sportswriters were out in full force that morning, moving from one man to the next, anxious to tackle Spike Russell as soon as he finished dressing. Not that they liked the job. This was a tough one to handle, the story of how one player had thoughtlessly jeopardized the chances of the Dodgers for the pennant.

The telephone rang. Old Chiselbeak answered. "Yeah . . . yeah . . . he is . . . yeah. He's in there with Draper and Fat Stuff now. O.K., I'll tell him." He went across the room, knocked at the door, and opened it. "Hey there, Spike. MacManus wants you. He wants to see you right away in his office."

Well, he thought, here goes. I intended to go up and tell him the whole thing myself as soon as I got rid of the reporters. But you can't keep things quiet long on a ballclub. Here goes, then. And this is one more time when being a manager is no fun.

The second he entered the luxurious room of the president, he realized trouble was ahead.

Like everyone connected with a major league club, Jack MacManus loved baseball. But first of all he was a businessman; he was not in there solely for the love of the game but to make money. Sport was one thing, and he was sincerely interested in sport; yet money was something else. And anything that interfered with a profit was apt to arouse his ire. Seated behind the big desk, clear and free of papers, he was puffing a large cigar, angrily blowing clouds of smoke into the air.

"Spike! I didn't wanna discuss this over the telephone. What seems to be the trouble with young Hathaway?"

"Jack . . . I . . . that is, we . . . that is . . . I've been having considerable trouble all summer with this boy Hathaway. He's kinda been a problem. 'Course he's a good pitcher, none better; and he's become hotter'n a firecracker as he got some good coaching from Charlie Draper and old Fat Stuff. They've really developed that lad between 'em. But all the time he was a pain in the neck for me. First of all, Jack, he injured his finger, you recall, and was laid off for several weeks. That was bad. Then he got to running round and, Jack, the fact is the boy got to drinking. He raised cain one night in St. Loo, so

I caught him and fined him fifty bucks. I warned him at the time, in fact I warned the whole club. I told 'em all as plainly as I could I wouldn't stand for any. . . ."

"Why, sure, I remember all that. I was for you, Spike; you gotta maintain discipline. I understand, but right now with the Cards here. . . ."

"Yes, but, Jack, wait a minute; lemme tell you the whole story. Then he cuts loose again, and I fine him a hundred bucks, and then in Chicago he goes haywire after pitching that shut-out and eats herring and bacon and eggs twelve days running for breakfast. Of course he gets sick. I overlooked that, just a fool stunt, though he was lost to us for almost a week. You know when a thing like that happens, and a man can't take his turn, it throws a burden on the other men on the pitching staff."

"Why sure, I know. I see how 'tis. But . . ."

"And then one night, in Pitt, I think it was, he went an' got gingered up, and had the telephone operator call everyone for a seven-thirty meeting in my room the next morning."

"Aw, what the hell! I heard about that. Why, Spike, he's only a crazy kid. You know how it is; you gotta expect things like that from these screwballs."

"Maybe so. Although I know what Grouchy Devine would have done to Bob and me if we'd ever pulled that one on the Vols. Anyhow, I talked to him. I explained how he'd bust up the sleep of the whole club. I warned him, Jack, his third time. I told him it would be the last time. I told him if he got into trouble again, I'd sure suspend him. The way he was pitching he could have been the rookie of the year if he'd only have steadied down. Then last night, before our big game, he goes out chasing this skirt, this what's-her-name up there at the Kit Kat Klub."

"How do you know?"

"I didn't know for sure. All I knew was he didn't roll in until some time after midnight. Then this morning, just by chance, Jim Casey happened to phone right while I was talking to him. Casey asked me point blank if he was the player seen last night at the Kit Kat Klub. I put it right up to Boney, and he admitted he was. What could I do? Three times . . . and out."

"Yeah . . . yeah . . . that's tough. I know how you feel . . . player disobey you like that . . . I unnerstand. . . ." He puffed nervously on his cigar and tapped it on the ashtray. No ashes fell off. They had fallen before in his excited movements, and dropped on the thick carpet on the

169

floor. "Yeah, O.K. The guy deserves it. I'd say he deserves it and you did just right. But for gosh sakes, Spike, look at the consequences."

"You tellin' me! Only baseball is built on discipline, Jack. I couldn't do anything else but suspend him, even were we due to go into the World Series tomorrow."

"But the team! Look at it from their viewpoint. The team'll be sore as hell at you; they'll . . ."

"No, they won't. They'll be sore at him. Remember it's Hathaway who's taking the money out of their pockets when he doesn't step out on that mound, not me. They all know what's happened; they know I've been patient with him. They'd like to go out and let loose, too, only they don't. You see they've been bearing down and he hasn't, and they darn well realize it."

"O.K. O.K., fine him. Fine him, Spike, fine him plenty. Give it to him with both barrels. Fine him a thousand bucks. But for goodness' sake don't suspend him; keep him in there working today."

"But, Jack, this is the third time. This has been going on since July. Ordinarily I'd be glad to keep him working. Not this time. He has it coming to him. Besides, he's hopping a plane for home. And that's all right with me."

Now Jack MacManus was furious. This was the last straw. The kid manager was stubborn. Recollections of previous clashes came to him; their battles over contracts, battles which Jack MacManus always won against other players because he held all the cards. Maybe he held them against Spike Russell, too; if so, he never played them right. Why, as his brother once said, "Spike's as stubborn as a North Carolina mule."

"Gone home! You let him get away! Listen, Spike! This means anywhere from four to six thousand bucks for every man on the club. They'll be down on you for life. You get that kid back, somehow, anyhow. If not, why, I couldn't keep you on as manager."

The shot struck home. Spike winced. But he replied quietly, firmly, with insistence.

"No, Jack, I'm not afraid of that. They won't be down on me; they'll be down on Bones Hathaway for quitting. Anyhow, I can't help it if they are. He's not coming back."

"Look, Spike." His tone was desperately persuasive now. "Frankly now, the Series would put the front office on easy street. We need that Series dough the worst way. It'd give us three-quarters of a million clear for working capital that we could use. With that we could go out next season and get you some top class kids to replace our veterans; we could pay off the bank mortgage; we could enlarge the place and build some new stands we need badly; we could . . ."

"Nosir, Jack, I just can't. I've already announced it, the newspapermen have put it on the wires by this time. And Bonesy is on his way home. Besides, no one man is indispensable to a ballclub. It's a lesson these kids all have to learn. Doggone, we'll win this thing without Hathaway; that's the kind of a ballclub it is. The tougher things get, the harder they fight. This'll put 'em on their mettle, you wait and see."

"You mean to stand there and tell me you can beat the Cards two out of three with Hathaway down in Tennessee?"

Silence fell over the room like a heavy fog. "Well . . . I'd say we gotta chance."

"Gotta chance! Gotta chance! Why, hang it all, you're throwing away the pennant, that's what you're doing. And the Series, too. You're costing the boys five-six thousand bucks apiece, and the club stands to lose half to three-quarters of a million. Yet you insist on ruining us . . . by being stubborn . . . by refusing to give in an inch . . . by . . ."

This was the MacManus that Spike Russell had always dreaded. He had seen the big fellow in rhubarbs with umpires, in disputes with officials of other clubs, or with the president of the League. Never had the Irishman's wrath been turned his way. Now it was on him, full blast. The red-faced man rose from the desk and, spluttering invective, shouting, growling, threatening, came forward.

Spike wavered before the storm; but he did not quit. He held his ground. Even when the irate magnate came round from behind his desk and walked close to him, shouting as loud as he could.

". . . Chucking away a pennant . . . that's just what you're doing . . . a million bucks into the bargain . . . for what? . . . a whim . . . a fancy . . . one million bucks. . . ." His voice was raised; he was shrieking now. "Looka here, Spike Russell! I hafta back you up on this; you released it to the papers. I can't change my manager now. But you just called the turn; one man isn't necessary to a ballclub, and you better think that over; you better get it out of your thick head that you are. If you persist . . . if you go ahead and ruin this team . . . I'll never give you another contract as long as you live. Nope, nor that kid brother of yours, either."

Spike saw the enraged face come close to his. There was much he wanted to say. But he didn't trust himself to reply. Instead he turned, opened the door, and walked out. His hand shook over the handle as he closed it. Going down the hall his knees were wobbly and he was trembling all over.

20

Was it the enormous crowd in the stands and the importance of the contest or the reaction from their long, stern chase or the suspension and departure of their star pitcher that made them slump that afternoon? Whatever it was, the Dodgers had the jitters. Old reliables like Harry Street bobbled easy grounders. Swanny juggled a single which was promptly stretched into a triple. Even Bob, with a runner trapped off second base, let a throw from Klein through into center field, and the man later scored.

Old Razzle felt this uneven support. He became wild and began passing men. Ordinarily pitchers don't mind walking a man, they have confidence in their ability to get the weaker hitters coming along. But now Razzle began to lose the next man also. This in turn reacted on the rest of the club. To the team behind the pitcher nothing is as demoralizing as bases on balls at critical moments. You can't do a thing about them. Outfielders paw the earth and walk around restlessly; infielders spit into their gloves and look nervously at each other from the corners of their eyes.

Fortunately the Cards were tight also that afternoon and ready to become panicky at the least chance. Like the Dodgers, they did their best to toss away the game. They, too, messed up easy chances, threw the ball wildly around the bases, missed opportunities at the plate. Both pitchers watched with agony from the box as runs were scored on careless mistakes in the field. This game on which so much depended, which should have been so close and tight, became a comedy of errors. Two apiece in the fourth; then the Cards scored twice and led four to two in the sixth. The Dodgers caught them and went ahead five to four in the seventh; but the Cards retaliated in the eighth when Clyde Baldwin, usually the steadiest of fielders, misjudged a fly. He first ran back for it, then saw it was falling short, came in, stabbed at it, and missed. The ball rolled through to the fence and three runs were over before Roy Tucker retrieved the ball.

"Shoot!" said Spike to Charlie Draper as they passed each other when the inning was over.

The coach, on his way to third base, paused. "Why, Spike, I couldn't believe my eyes. I didn't even get up off my seat in the dugout, I was so sure he had it. He never did that before, never."

But there it was, and the score seven to five going into the eighth. The Dodgers managed to pick up two runs by forcing the Cards to throw the ball round the diamond, and should have had another. But Red Allen was called out on a grounder which he beat into third by a foot. The decision was so raw it brought the entire dugout to the step, while a howl rose from the fans back of third base. Red Allen, quiet and even-tempered, went to pieces. He stormed up to Stubblebeard behind the bag, protesting violently. The old man folded his arms and turned away. The decision stood.

At the start of the ninth the Cards worked a man to third with one out. The next batter hit an easy fly, and Roy Tucker stood under it waiting, thumping his glove as usual, while the ball dropped. Before he had it the man on third was off to the plate, and with a desperate slide beat Roy's perfect throw to Jocko Klein. This time Spike roared out of the dugout, Charlie Draper at his side.

"Why, Stubblebeard, he was out from here to breakfast!"

"Man, you saw; he was at least four feet offa that bag before Tuck had the ball in his mitt."

"Shoot, Stubble, you know darn well he left that base before the ball was caught, you know that. . . ."

The umpire was surrounded by a noisy, angry mob of players, everyone shrieking at him. The stands were howling also for everyone had seen the runner break before the ball was caught. But once again the umpire was firm. His decision was made. In vain the Dodgers protested, appealed to the plate umpire. The Cards were ahead, eight to seven.

Once more the Dodgers had to pull up, to come from behind. A game team, as usual they made the effort. Harry Street struck out; but Bob drilled a clean one into center field. The stands watched as Jocko Klein went up to the plate.

Would the manager try for a tie or try to win? Would he order his catcher to bunt or hit straightaway? With the St. Louis bullpen going furiously into action, he played boldly for victory, and Jocko, hitting behind the runner with a clean drive into right, vindicated his judgment. Now there were men on first and third, one out, and the winning run on the bases, as Clyde Baldwin, the Brooks' slugger, came to bat.

Grouchy chose to pitch to him and, walking out to the mound, waved in a left-hander to relieve. The Card pitcher took his time coming from the bullpen, and Grouchy stood conferring with a group that consisted of his catcher, his third baseman, and the second baseman and captain of the club. Razzle, ready for a laugh even in the tensest moment, sauntered out with a bat in his hand and joined the circle. He put one arm around the shoulder of the catcher, inclined his head and listened. The crowd yelled with delight. Then Grouchy looked up and saw Razzle. The conference fell apart. The crowd yelled and Raz retreated, pleased with himself.

Clyde Baldwin tapped the plate nervously. "Now, then, Clyde. Unbutton your shirt, Clyde. Le's have a hit, Clyde. Bring those babies home, Clyde, old kid. . . ."

Clyde waited the full count. With the runners set and poised, he swung and popped weakly to the shortstop. Two out.

Spike searched in the rack for his favorite bat. "Where's that Black Betsy of mine . . . here . . . nope . . . yes, here it is. . . ." Now then, it's up to me. Clyde fell down, but I'll pick him up. I'll bring that kid brother of mine home if it's the last thing I do on earth. I'm gonna bring him in with that run, I sure am. . . .

The first ball was an inside, medium fast ball, a ball the pitcher tried to sneak over for a strike. Spike got hold of it and socked it hard between first and second. The ball was past, it was through, it rolled joyously into the field, as Klein in a dust cloud roared into third, and Bob galloped over with the tying run. They were still alive.

Hold on! From the sack where he stood panting, Spike's heart sank. Old Grouchy was lumbering out from the Cardinal dugout. Grouchy never took the field save in an emergency, and Spike instantly knew his presence there meant trouble. Now what? The manager was talking to the umpire. From first base Spike could hear those sharp, familiar tones as he spoke to the umpire beside the plate.

"Give those birds a dose of Rule 44, Section I, Stubble." The umpire pulled a piece of white paper from his pocket. It was the Dodger batting order. He took one look and administered the bitter dose. Two days previously Spike had shaken up his batting order. In the confusion and excitement of the moment, he had gone to bat instead of Razzle who should have followed Klein. The pitcher was so pleased with his feat of kidding the Cardinal board of strategy, that he, also, failed to realize Spike was batting out of turn. Consequently the manager was out under the rules; the run he had driven in didn't count. The game was over. The Cards had won.

You've only got yourself to blame when a thing of this kind happens. And yet . . . if only Raz hadn't given those two bases on balls in the eighth; if only the big showboat hadn't tried to act up in the ninth; if Swanny hadn't juggled that single in the fourth; if Clyde had been playing his usual game; most of all if the Hathaway thing hadn't upset him so he mixed up his batting turn. Then, too, if those vital decisions hadn't gone against them. Those decisions were what cost the game.

The pay-off came later. He was leaving the park when at the exit a hand reached out and drew him to one side. It was Stubblebeard. Spike noticed for the first time the hollow places under the old man's eyes, and the deep, sunken cheeks. Why, maybe umps didn't sleep nights, either.

"Spike, boy, I realize this isn't doing you any good; it isn't doing anyone any good but me. I just want you to know I was wrong on both those decisions out there. I've made a lotta bad ones in my time; but them two was the worst. Only, see, I couldn't change 'em on the field. It would have looked too raw. That's how the business is. . . ."

There was something in the old fellow's tone and twisted face that made Spike forget even the rawness of the defeat that hung over him. He held out his hand and reached for Stubblebeard's.

"Why, shucks, Stubble, don't you let that worry you. I know; I understand. I realize you couldn't change before all that crowd out there. But I'm mighty obliged to you for speaking about it; that helps, Stubble, that helps lots. Now you go home and get yourself a good rest tonight. We'll see you out there tomorrow, hear me?"

21

For once Jack MacManus sat back and let someone else do the talking. His few words were brief and pointed.

"Well, I'll be damned . . . izzat so? Well . . . he did . . . the dirty crook!" And he sat back puffing furiously on his cigar in the parlor of his hotel suite. For once Jack MacManus was allowing someone else to do the talking.

Bob Russell was doing the talking. He was excited, too, and pleased with himself as he watched the president's expression change. "But even then I didn't really think anything; I mean, I wasn't sure. Until I remembered that line of Hanson's in Pittsburgh, like I told you when he was talking to Chisel that afternoon. And I remembered he was always kinda knocking Spike behind his back, kinda, well, you know. . . ."

"And I trusted that rat, too."

"An' so I beat it up to Hathaway's room as soon as you rang off. Bonesy is packing up to go home; he's suspended. What for? ' 'Cause I went up to the Kit Kat,' he says. 'What d'ja do that for?' I ask him. 'For Baldwin,' he tells me. Now these two boys came up together; they usta be roomies on the club and they're pals. So when he hears Baldwin is off on the loose, naturally he wants to go find him. But wait a minute. 'How d'ja know he was up there?' I ask him. Then comes the pay-off. 'Why, Hanson told me last night. Hanson found he wasn't in his room.' Get it?"

"The lousy so-and-so! The big crook!" Jack MacManus' cigar blew smoke like a factory chimney.

"Then off he piles for his plane before I could stop him. Like that; he's gone. So I try to find Baldwin. No Baldwin. Or Harry Street, his roommate. No Harry, either. Finally I get to the field just before noon. Spike isn't there; he's up with you. But I get Street to one side and ask about Baldwin. 'Naw,' says Harry. 'Baldwin came in at nine and never left the room all night.' Get it? Hanson, as plain . . ."

"Why, that bum . . . that . . ."

"Wait now. Then directly the game's over, I see Casey. How did Casey get wind of it? Hanson again. He tells me he gets the tip-off from Bill in the lobby this morning while Spike is dressing down Hathaway. So Casey, he calls Spike and naturally asks who's on the loose at the Kit Kat last night. Spike falls just as Hanson intended he should, and turns on Bonesy. 'Were you up at the Kit Kat last night?' 'Sure I was there,' says Bonesy, thinking only to save Baldwin, and won't tell why."

For once MacManus was speechless.

"That ain't all. I'm piecing things together like Sherlock Holmes himself. It's Hanson this and Hanson that and Hanson here and Hanson there, so I figure maybe it wasn't either Bonesy or Baldwin who staged that phony meeting in our room early that morning. Finally I get the phone girl who was on duty that night. She shows me the written slip she had with the message to wake up everyone at seven-thirty except the two kids. It's on Hanson's typewriter, and what's more it isn't signed. Get it?"

"I get it. I get a lot more you don't know about. Things that have been reported to me over the long distance from Cinci and St. Loo and Pittsburgh. That rat! He'd even wreck the club if it got him a good job."

"He darn near succeeded. As it was, he cost us this game today. We could have won that easy with Bonesy out there."

MacManus blew clouds of smoke into mid-air. "We'll have him for tomorrow. Bob, you've done a good job on this. You sure used your bean. And I won't forget it when next year's contract comes up, either." He reached for the telephone, fumbling with a little black notebook in his hand.

"Long distance . . . I want Hathaway . . . J.B. in . . . in . . . Jefferson City, Tennessee. . . . I don't know if it is in his name or not . . . anyhow get him . . . that's right . . . that's it . . . this is fourteen sixty-six."

There was a knock at the door. Bob went over to open it and found his brother. The older Russell was by far the more astonished of the two.

Jack MacManus banged down the phone and jumped from his seat, puffing clouds of smoke as he rose. He came across the sitting room of his suite and, grabbing his young manager by the arm, led him to the big davenport.

"Spike! I wanted you to know firsthand from me the whole story on this. Your brother Bob has uncovered a mighty dangerous situation. There's been dirty work going on in this club right under my eyes, and that rat Hanson almost got away with it. First of all, I want to say to you I'm ashamed of myself the way I talked to you at the clubhouse this morning. I didn't know the facts. I'm sorry I acted the way I did; please forget the whole thing."

Spike Russell was just about the most puzzled man in Brooklyn. A call from the operator had ordered him to report to MacManus' suite. He came up as the manager of a beaten team, a team that had just dropped a critical game because he himself had lost his presence of mind. He came also as a discharged ball-player; he came up bewildered and sore and disappointed. To find his brother with Jack MacManus.

It wasn't the MacManus he had left that morning, either; red, angry, loud. It was a MacManus in a rare mood; subdued and apologetic.

"Spike, I'm ashamed I lost my temper. You

handled this thing swell; you played by the book and you were dead right. Only you were up against the biggest double-crosser in baseball!"

Still Spike Russell was confused. He knew things had changed, that he was not fired; but he couldn't quite understand what had happened.

"As for Hanson," continued MacManus, "he's through. He's out. He's out of baseball forever. I'll take good care of that. Your brother Bob here has saved us all. That is, if we can get Bonesy back. And we will, if we have to charter a special plane. I'm thoroughly ashamed of myself for carrying on the way I did to a guy who's been taking it as you have ever since the middle of July. I want you to know I'm for you all the way; win, lose or draw."

"Gee . . . that helps, Jack, that really helps."

"And don't think I don't mean what I say. Those aren't just words, Spike. You come up to the office before that game tomorrow, and you can sign a three-year contract with a ten grand raise. You've done a swell job for us this season." The telephone jangled. MacManus was over and on it with two jumps.

"Yeah . . . yeah . . . uhuh . . . put him on, put him on, will ya? Uhuh." The cigar waggled furiously in his mouth. "Bonesy! That you,

Bones?" he shouted. "That you, Bonesy? Listen now, we want you back. Never mind that . . . oh, we straightened that out O.K. You grab yourself the first plane you can from Knoxville tonight . . . no, not tomorrow . . . tonight, d'ya hear me? . . . tonight . . . tonight . . . tonight. . . ."

22

He waited while they settled themselves around him as he stood, one knee on the bench before him. The thought suddenly wrenched his heart that this could be the last meeting of the year; but he put it quickly away and looked at them all, the boys in the back, the friendly faces in the rear and down front, at Fat Stuff with his arm around Jocko Klein, his former roomie. The old pitcher's World Series ring caught Spike's attention. It was gold, with a red border and a diamond triangle in the center. A gleam of light caught the diamond and made it sparkle.

"Close that door, Chisel. O.K., boys. Seems

like a mistake has been made. By this time you all prob'ly know what's happened. One player was unjustly penalized for something he didn't do. O.K., this has been taken care of; the suspension on Bones Hathaway has been lifted. He left Knoxville last night by plane. The weather's sort of settling in, but we hope to have him out there on the mound by game time.

"Now this thing has been squared off; it's gone now, it's over, forget it. Forget it, every one of you. Le's us all go out there and fight. Remember, Grouchy plays the percentages. He never goes overboard being too smart. No need to discuss their hitters again. Just don't forget that Mac Ennis is an opposite field hitter, and a difficult man to throw to. Danaher likes a ball he can pull; give him one and sure as shooting he'll hit it where you ain't. Stan Frankel is deceptive. He's a clumsy batter; he can't get out of the way of the ball high inside. We like to pitch tight to him, but we're afraid to because the ball hits him. O.K. . . . any questions? All right . . . every man play his position up to the hilt—and beyond. Le's go!"

Clack-clack, clackety-clack, clack-clack, clackety-clack . . . the team turned, poured out the door to take the field. As they came out into the bright sunshine, the mass of blue shirts and white shirts in the sunny bleachers was a speckled blotch of popcorn to their eyes. And round and above was the hum of the thousands filling the stands, while from every side came the sounds of baseball. Especially those metallic voices to be heard in every park in every city in the league.

"... Score card ... score card ... can't tell the players without a score card ... fresh roasted peanuts ... get 'em ice cold ... ice cold soda ... you can't tell the players without a score card ... anyone else here wanna score card. ..."

As Spike passed the St. Louis dugout he observed Grouchy talking to a sportswriter. The old man's familiar voice could be heard, the same contemptuous tone he always used on sportswriters.

"The hot corner! The hot corner! What's hot about it? I could play it with my legs crossed. A third baseman stands all afternoon in the shade; maybe he handles two-three chances if he's busy. Why, anyone can play third base."

Spike glanced at Harry Street beside him. Harry shook his head. "Guess Grouchy thinks third base is a wart that oughta be removed.

Well, maybe. I only wish he had to stand up to some of those drives of Danaher's, though."

"Aw, Grouchy, he's always like that. He doesn't mean anything; it's his line."

Before long they were taking the field. There was tension all over the park. No wonder, for every ball that afternoon had a price tag attached. On that tag was the cash difference between winning and losing the pennant, between the Series and a chance at six thousand dollars or second place and a few hundred. No wonder the Dodgers were nervous as they warmed up; no wonder they watched the entrance to the dugout for signs of Bones Hathaway. Game time drew near. A thick blanket of cloud hung low over the field, and it was apparent to everyone he wouldn't start. As the umpires stepped to the plate, the team was still without their star pitcher, so Elmer McCaffrey took the mound.

He might come, though, any minute, in time to relieve Elmer. But Elmer pitched steady ball. In the third Splinter Danaher hit an easy rolling grounder toward Spike. He was charging in when, to his horror, Elmer dashed over from the box and deflected the ball away from him. Like all good infielders, Spike timed his stride, and this interception meant he had to change his timing. When he reached the ball the runner was steaming into first and a throw was useless. Through no one's fault an easy out was turned into a scratchy safety.

Mac Ennis, the Card slugger, came swinging his war club to the plate. Elmer stepped off the mound and stood rubbing up the ball with his hands. He appeared to be looking toward the bench, but he was really looking where every man on the team was looking, to see if Bonesy was there. Then he stuffed his shirt into his trousers, throwing up his arms above his head to give himself clearance in the most uncomfortable costume ever devised by man, and stepped into the box. He took Klein's signal, glanced over toward the runner on first, and threw.

"Ball one."

Again he looked round, checked the runner and pitched. Ennis gave it everything he had, and the ball rifled through the box. Then from nowhere came Spike Russell, gloved hand outstretched in a dizzy dive. Somehow he reached the ball as it sizzled back of second, knocked it down and stabbed it in the dirt. He was off balance, but not content with having stopped it from going through, he made a desperate backhand flip to his brother waiting on second. Bob stood there, feet braced, knees apart, waiting to get the ball.

Ninety feet. Thirty yards from base to base. Thirty yards, which a fast man can do in a little over three seconds. Three seconds from the moment in which the ball is struck to beat the batter to first. Bob caught the ball the only possible way, spearing it in mid-air, then leaping those dangerous spikes as they flashed in, and shooting it with every ounce of strength behind his tough, young arm. The umpire near first threw one hand behind his head. A doubleplay, and a rally nipped at the start.

The game went on, the clouds descended lower and lower, and still Bonesy didn't show up. Yet Elmer was pitching good ball; he was ahead of the hitters, and for the most part the Cards could do nothing with him. However the Card pitcher was throwing shut-out ball also. The Dodgers weren't hitting, either. They were tight at the plate. But speed came to their rescue. Leslie Stevens, one of the best catchers in the business, found he couldn't afford to wait the fraction of a second for the umpire's call on a fourth ball. If he did and it was a strike, the runner on first had a start no throw on earth could beat.

In the seventh, with the game still a scoreless tie, Clyde Baldwin came to bat. Once again speed helped, speed that in sport is first cousin to daring. There was one man out when Clyde smashed a long clothesline into the gap between right and center field. The diamond dissolved into motion. Clyde took his turn around first, tore into second and, getting the sign from Draper, came roaring into third as the Cardinal fielder reached the ball in deep center. For the first time the Dodgers had a man in scoring position.

Roy Tucker, following, immediately delivered with a fly ball, a lazy can of corn deep toward the fence that the leftfielder had to back up for, so far back that he didn't even try to make the throw to the plate. Clyde came across with a run, the first of the game.

That run looked bigger and bigger as the game went on and still no Bonesy appeared in the dugout. In the eighth two Cards struck out and the third popped to Bob. In the ninth, with a one-run lead, the Dodgers were only three precarious put-outs from triumph. Yet those Cards were a dead-game club. Dusty Miller, the first batter, smacked a drive that Swanny stopped but couldn't handle cleanly. Dusty tore for second. The ball was retrieved too late for Bob on second to get Miller. The umpire, standing almost over them, threw out his palms. Instantly Bob jumped back of him.

"Yer out!" he shouted.

Miller, engulfed in the storm of dust over his head, heard the muffled tones above, thought it was the umpire, scrambled to his feet and charged over. Bob simply reached out and tagged him. This time the Card runner was out and no mistake.

The fans yelled, the fans shrieked, the fans booed and catcalled. They loved it. They went wild with delight; they jeered at Miller; their roars echoed from the bleachers to the home plate and back again; they pursued the luckless Cardinal into the obscurity of the dugout. Then suddenly that Niagara of noise died away, Tom Weston, the Cardinal shortstop, hit one through the hole between first and second.

The team spit into their gloves and looked anxiously toward the dugout for signs of their star pitcher. But no Bonesy appeared, and out in the bullpen Rog Stinson and Rats Doyle began warming up. Spike hitched at his belt, leaned over to pick up a pebble from the basepath, pawed at the dirt under his feet, thinking what they were all thinking—if only Bones would come. Meanwhile the man at bat glanced over toward Grouchy in the dugout for the hit or take sign. The old chap was foxy. Spike knew him well enough to realize he would cross them up if he could. That meant he'd probably order the hit and run.

He did. On the second pitch the batter struck solidly behind the runner, a clean drive into right again. Smart fielding by Swanny held the Cards to first and second; but now the winning run was on the bases. Spike felt the team watching him, waiting to see whether he would go along with Elmer or bring in a new pitcher. He walked across to the mound, stalling, hoping that a delay of a few minutes would somehow make Bonesy appear. He came up to the big pitcher and smiled. The hurler nodded.

"O.K., Spike, I'll get this man for you."

The manager patted him on the arm. "Keep 'em low, Elmer; the old doubleplay ball, you know . . . throw him your hook."

Elmer agreed, stepped off the rubber, took the sign and stepped in. Connolly dropped the first ball in front of the plate, a perfect bunt that rolled gently away from Klein, away from everyone toward third. But Elmer was expecting just that. Like a flash the big man darted after the ball, picked it up and, turning, saw Ennis slide into third. So he instantly whirled and shot it to Red on first. Man and ball arrived exactly together, for the Cards were fast, too.

A roar went up over the field as the runner flashed by first base. It was a strange and curious roar, a roar that didn't die away but grew louder and louder and louder, a roar that seemed to pull the fans to their feet, shrieking. For a minute Spike, watching the decision at first anxiously, was confused. So were other men on the team. Then they all saw it together.

Bones Hathaway was throwing beside the dugout to Charlie Draper.

Spike saw him just as Elmer did, and Red on first, and Roy Tucker with his hands on his hips in deep center, and Harry Street astride third base. There he was; not throwing in his calm and leisurely way; but fast, faster, faster, with no windup at all, burning in the ball to the coach with the catcher's mitt.

The crowd kept on yelling. They yelled and yelled, while the runners stood poised on the bases and no one moved.

At last Elmer turned and looked at Spike. The manager walked across. He walked slowly, as slowly as he could, and all the time Bones was steaming in those pitches to Draper and the crowd was shrieking. Elmer walked slowly off the mound toward the dugout.

"Hathaway, number 15, now pitching for Brooklyn. . . ."

But the announcer's words were lost in the roar over the field as Bones, tossing in his last pitch to Draper, came out toward the diamond. He gave Elmer a slap on the arm as they passed, and took the ball from him. Then he stepped on the rubber and threw in another pitch, and another, and another. While Spike looked anxiously around, at the outfield playing slightly toward left, at his infield with Red and Harry well over toward the foul lines to cut possible two baggers, at Ennis standing in foul territory below third so as not to be hit by a batted ball, at Stan Frankel coming to the plate. It was up to Bonesy.

At last he was ready. The storm clouds were lower now, and the field was getting darker rapidly. An ideal spot for a fast-ball pitcher if only he had control. Even the bullpen paused to watch the rookie in the test before him. Frankel stood there menacingly; Frankel, the clumsy, dangerous batter, the man you had to watch.

Bones took the sign and threw.

"Ball one!"

The crowd on its feet shouted nervously. Even Grouchy in the dugout became excited. He stood on the step clapping his hands together, almost an emotional outburst for that unemotional figure. The coaches behind first and third yelled through their hands, and the runners danced up and down the baselines as Bonesy threw again.

"Ball two!"

Spike came over. Bones leaned down, touched the dirt with his fingers, picked up the rosin bag, and brushed off his manager. He stood there in that howling, insane mob, the coolest person on the field.

"Strike!"

The roar rose as Frankel watched a perfect one cut the plate. He shook his head, looked round at Stubblebeard, glanced over at Grouchy for the hit or take sign. Then he waved his bat, an ominous sign.

Bones didn't wait. He threw again, and this

time Frankel swung hard. But well underneath the ball. Two and two. Jocko snapped it back to Bonesy and knelt down to give the sign, while the runners still danced on the basepaths, arms waving, darting back and forth, ready to run as the pitcher threw.

Once more it was a daring pitch to the weakness of the batter, high and inside, close to his chest. Frankel swung from his heels with all he had and missed the ball by a foot.

Then Jocko with the right side open, hardly changing his stance, rifled it to first. The ball came hard and low to the bag where the Card runner was scuttling desperately back. In one movement Red nabbed the throw and, sweeping round, slapped it on him as he tried to slide in to safety. The game was over.

23

The last game. The last game of all and the pennant depending upon it. Two fighting teams fighting right up to the wire. In every newspaper in the nation sportswriters hastily thumbed through baseball guides to see when it had happened before. They went back to 1940 when Detroit won the final game of the season against Cleveland; yes, and to 1942 when the Cards didn't clinch things until the last afternoon of the season. Here was the same situation, the pennant hanging on that last game of all.

In the dressing room Spike stood before the

team that had fought with him all season, the men who had come from behind, who had picked themselves up off the floor not once but a dozen times since he took over in July. What a gang! I'd rather lose with these boys than win with the Yanks. I said that before, and I mean it. Well, here goes. . . .

"I'm gonna make this short today. I wanna get out there and I'm sure you do, too. Everyone knows what depends on this one. We've been over their hitters. Nothing more to say. This-here pitcher, this man Rackenbusch, has won twenty games; but he has to throw a round ball the same as you fellas, and get it over the same platter. It's true he beat us in St. Loo the last time; you'll all remember he needed every bit of luck in the world to do it. Luck's on our side now. One thing, these Cards are a hitting club and hitting clubs pick up the marbles. We aren't a team of sluggers, and sometimes I notice the boys laugh at us and call us lucky. Point is we score runs. That's what counts. The only thing in baseball, as I see it, is to get more runs than the other guys, no matter how you get 'em. That's what we did yesterday. I'm convinced we'll do it again today. O.K. then, everyone play his position up to the hilt. Le's us grab off that pennant."

Instead of dissolving into the customary storm of scraping benches and conversation and the usual noise of spikes on wood and concrete, they sat still. Only old Fat Stuff stood.

"Spike, we . . . that is the boys here . . . all wanted me to say this. We won yesterday and pulled even with those Redbirds. And we're not a-going to look back. Today we intend to win this for you, Spike."

Then they broke up, everyone talking at once. "This one is for Spike." "Le's get this one for Spike." He stood watching, listening. Gosh, what a gang! Yes, sir, I'd lose with these boys any day rather than win with the Yanks.

On the field you instantly felt the importance of the contest. It was only one-thirty; but the stands were already more than half filled and, below, the space around the dugouts and behind the plate was crowded with strangers. Men he'd never seen before stood beside the batting cage, reporters and sportswriters from what seemed like every newspaper in the nation stayed at his elbow, pestering him with questions, keeping on him so he hardly had a moment to take his cut at the plate. Klein passed by with his tools under one arm. Spike beckoned and leaned over.

"Jocko, watch that signal catching a runner off second. Watch me closely on that; for a second I thought you were going to throw down to me yesterday. And that throw in the third . . ."

"Spike, that was the darned worst heave I ever made in my life. Know what happened?"

"Sure, I know. You slipped just as you threw. Don't worry; I've seen Bill Dickey chuck that ball into center field occasionally. You know, Jocko, I b'lieve you get more steam on your throw and you get it off faster, like that one in the ninth yesterday, than any catcher in this league."

"Do you? Do you really, Spike? Thanks lots." Someone called his name and the catcher took his place in the cage back of the plate.

"Mr. Russell. Hey, would you mind, would you mind stepping over this way just a minute?"

"What for? I bet I posed twenty times shaking hands with him yesterday." Spike knew what the cameramen wanted. The same old thing.

"Just once today, please, Spike." So he walked across to the Cardinal dugout where Grouchy was standing with his back turned. As he approached, he saw some brash reporter come up with a smile and extended hand. Evidently someone who doesn't know the old man, thought Spike to himself.

"Good morning, Grouchy," said the stranger pleasantly.

Grouchy looked at him, at the extended hand to which he paid no attention. "What's good about it?" he asked gruffly. Then, turning, he saw Spike and the photographers approaching. "Are you pests after me again?"

But he posed nevertheless. He had to pose and he knew it. That's as much a part of being a manager as running a team on the field. They stood there for the kneeling circle of cameramen, shaking hands, looking at each other, the boy who had come up from the minors to lead the Dodgers, and the old man who had taught and trained him. The ordeal was finished at last. Then a bell rang. The Dodgers dashed out on the field for practice. Finally this, too, was over. They came slowly in, the plate was brushed off, the basepaths swept, and Charlie Draper went up to old Stubblebeard with the batting order in his hand. There were four umpires on the diamond, showing how important every decision was to be.

Then from above came the loudspeaker.

". . . Batteries for today's game. . . . For St. Louis . . . Rackenbusch, pitching, Stevens, catching. For Brooklyn, Hathaway, pitching, Klein . . ."

But you couldn't hear the last words. The crowd made too much noise.

24

Goose eggs all the way. Goose eggs on the scoreboard in deep right every inning. Goose eggs up as they went into the sixth, the seventh, the eighth. Shadows lengthened, edged closer and closer to third base, gradually encroached upon the diamond itself; on Bones in the box, raising his arms to loosen his shirt in that familiar pitcher's gesture, on Roy Tucker thumping his glove in center, on Jocko Klein on his toes behind the plate, on Spike in deep short, nerves tight, now hitching at his belt, now scraping a pebble from the basepath and tossing it away, now rubbing his hand across the chest of his shirt or pawing at the dirt with his spikes.

So into the ninth with the teams tied and the issue of the pennant still in doubt. Then it happened, after two Cards went down in succession and Bones appeared to have them eating from his hand. It happened, as always in baseball, when you least expected it. First the young pitcher missed Miller and gave him a walk. He was letting the Cards look at his fast one, which he frequently wasted at the start, and then coming in for a change of pace. It fooled them because they were over-anxious and consequently just a trifle off in their timing. But he shoved that over once too often. Leslie Stevens wasn't fooled. Perhaps Grouchy on the bench wasn't fooled. Anyway the Cardinal catcher caught the ball squarely. The result was a long drive that bounced against the fence. The run was over and Stevens came into third standing.

The next man struck out, but the damage was done. Defeat was there with them in the last of the ninth, there in the dugout facing them all. On the steps Spike walked back and forth, urging every man, shaking them up, getting pinch hitters ready. Swanny was the first batter.

Swanny hit hard but the ball went directly at Tom Weston near second. Old Iceberg fielded the ball cleanly and retired Swanny at first. Red

Allen, the next man, ducked to avoid a duster. The ball hit his bat and soared gently into short left out of everyone's reach. He reached first safely.

The stands roared; hope was revived; the Brooks were in again fighting. Roy Tucker, three for nothing, came up due to deliver. He waited cautiously, looked at two bad ones, fouled off a couple of pitches, and then bashed a solid single to the right field wall. Red went sliding and rolling into third and there were men on first and third and only one out. Yes, the Brooks were still in the game.

The Cards thought so, too, and a feverish activity began in their bullpen in left as Bob Russell came to the plate. He hit a wicked hopper but Gus Connolly on third stopped it cold. Instead of throwing to first, he caught Red halfway down the basepath. From the dugout Spike watched with anguish in his heart as the Cards closed in relentlessly; Gus to Stevens to Gus to Stevens and back again to Gus who dashed after Red and slapped the ball on him for the out.

Two out. Only one man left, one man from defeat. With despair Spike watched Harry at the plate. Just keep us going, Harry; keep us in there, keep us alive somehow, anyhow. You're a clutch hitter, Harry. You aren't a powerhouse like some of those sluggers, but you sure come through in the pinches. Save us, Harry old boy, save us this time. . . .

The third sacker was a cool customer. He watched one ball and fouled off another. Then came a ball. And a third. The pitcher slipped over a strike. One strike from defeat. Bob, perched on first base, was yelling through cupped hands.

"The big one left, Harry, old timer, the big one left!"

From the circle where he waited Spike hardly dared watch. Harry stood there coolly as the ball came in low to the side. He flung away his bat and walked to first. The bases were filled.

Spike was so weak his knees actually trembled; he felt completely unequal to the job of winning the game. But he gripped his bat and stood there, while Grouchy came slowly out. A new pitcher. Slowly another man came in from the bullpen, the crowd clap-clapping. This was the time to win the game.

The field was darker now and gloomier. But it didn't seem to help the newcomer. His first two pitches were wide as the big crowd howled with delight. A low ball came that Stubble called a strike. Then another ball. Spike saw he was nervous, not yet warmed up completely. The fourth ball came, the run was over, the score was tied.

Bones Hathaway came slowly to the plate, watching Spike on first. Should he relieve him or not; slide in Paul Roth or stay with the rookie? By gosh, he's not a bad hitter; I'm gonna stay with him. He's still fresh, and he's the best man we got out there in that box. So Bonesy slowly and hesitatingly came to the plate.

He caught the first ball, and there was violence behind the blow. It was a long hit, a terrific shot between left and center, and the runners were off as they heard the sound of the bat. Spike charging toward second had the whole scene before him; Frankel and Danaher running vainly for it, the ball in the slot between them. Then Frankel with a burst of speed reached out with one hand as the ball roared past and speared it in mid-air. Danaher sheered away to avoid a collision, tripped and rolled over and over on the thick turf of the field.

The fans had to recognize the play that had robbed them of the game. They gave Frankel a great hand; they forced him to touch his cap again and again as he came in toward the dugout. As for Spike, he was so happy to be still in there fighting, so happy to be running back to his place in the field instead of returning disconsolately to the showers, that the failure to win the game right there was immediately forgotten.

Now we'll really get those guys.

Bones in fine form set the Cards down in the top of the tenth, and the Dodgers went out in order in their half. The top of the eleventh was hitless for the invaders, the bottom equally so for the Dodgers. There was trouble in the twelfth. With two down, Bones walked a batter and the next man scratched an infield hit. Then Danaher came across with his third safety, a hot liner to left field.

With two gone the runner on second was off and hustling hard for home as the blow was struck. But Clyde, too, started with the sound of the bat. Straining, giving everything, running madly, he charged in. There was a race between ball and fielder. By sheer speed he managed to grab it on the first hop, then without pausing threw to the plate. The throw was perfect and the runner cut down by a foot. Had Clyde waited to take it normally on the second bounce, the Cards would have had another one-run lead.

The fans were still yelling when Bob swung up to the plate in the Brooks' half of the twelfth. That noise did him good. He singled solidly to center and there was a man on first and no one out. Harry Street followed, and set them back by swinging on three pitched balls. Spike came up, tapped the rubber twice, knocked the dirt from his spikes with the heel of his bat, tugged at his cap, and stood watching the pitcher who was rubbing up the ball, checking the runner, taking the sign and nodding to his catcher.

It was a low ball and he met it in front of the plate. That was all he saw, that and his brother roaring, head down, toward second. He felt the catcher's throw behind his ear just as he stepped on the bag. He was out, but Bob was on second in scoring position. He walked slowly back to the bench, with that same decision again before him. Bones was sauntering slowly up to the plate, while on the steps of the dugout stood Paul Roth and Alan Whitehouse, swinging bats in their hands.

No, sir. No, sir. I'm gonna stick with Bonesy all the way. He's got a right to win his own game, and he darned near did it for us in the ninth. I've stuck with my pitchers all season in times like this, and I'm not gonna change my style of baseball in the last game of the year. He walked slowly in and wedged himself beside old Fat Stuff, with half the team on the steps calling for a hit. Two out, and the fastest second baseman in the league in scoring position.

Bones took the first one. Shoot, thought Spike, that was a pip. A fast ball right across. There was the ballgame riding on that one. Now he'll give him a change of pace most likely.

Bones walked away, scooped up some dirt and rubbed it on his palms, tapped his spikes, and resumed his place in the box. The next pitch was not a change of pace; it was a hook, low and slightly wide.

To Spike's amazement he heard the voice of Stubblebeard behind the plate.

"Steerike tuh . . ."

A jeer rose from the stands instantly. For a second the boy at bat stood motionless. Then something seized him. Bones Hathaway, the quiet Bones, the pitcher who never engaged in rhubarbs on the field, who always let Draper and the coaches carry on the arguments, suddenly went wild.

"Strike!" He turned back. "Whazzat . . . you

called that a strike?" He dropped his bat and stood beside the old umpire, and his voice carried to the dugout. "Hey, there, Stubble, what's the matter with your eyesight these days? . . . Why, that ball was a foot outside. . . ."

This was enough for the crowd. They rocked and roared above and around him, they supported him to a man, they whistled and catcalled, they stormed and shrieked and shouted disapproval. The ancient umpire shifted his chest protector with his elbows and kept his gaze fixed firmly on the pitcher standing motionless in the box.

"You blind, Stubble, or what? It was bad enough the other day . . . without you have to hang it on us again."

The blue-clad figure took off his mask, held it in one hand, and turned away. He took three or four steps toward the stands; the stands on their feet, howling for his blood. This man was an enemy of Brooklyn. Bones followed at his heels, pouring invective on him. Suddenly the umpire wheeled around.

Spike Russell jumped from the dugout followed by Charlie Draper. They saw trouble in the way the old man turned, and they heard his voice plainly. "One more word, Hathaway, and you're through for the day. I mean that, and don't think I'm foolin'. One more word. . . ."

The old chap's tone yanked Bones from his anger. He stood silent, uncertain for a minute as he saw his manager and coach rush toward him. Then, smothering his resentment as well as he could, he turned back to the plate, took his club from the bat boy, and stepped into the box. To his surprise he was trembling all over. He got ready. Nothing and two. Two strikes and no balls.

The next pitch was a duster, directly at his head. Angry now, his reflexes were slow. He had trouble dodging the ball, and it sent him sprawling foolishly back into the dirt, his bat clattering from his hand. The fall was so unexpected it shook him badly. This made him more angry than ever. He took his time rising, got up slowly, slapping dust from his uniform.

Maybe I made a mistake, thought Spike. Maybe I should have put in a pinch hitter; maybe the kid can't take it. Yep, it looks as if I guessed wrong. It looks as if I made a mistake.

"Oh-oh. That's bad; that's really bad." Old Fat Stuff on the bench beside him shook his head. "I know that boy Hathaway. That pitcher couldn't have done anything worse. He'll be right sorry he threw that duster, you wait and see. Oh, that's bad, that is."

The next one was inside. A ball. Two and two. Again the rookie pitcher took a toehold as the pitch came. It was a medium high fast ball, and he caught it squarely. You could tell by the sound this was a hard blow. In exactly the same place, the slot between left and center, but this time a shot that cleared the outstretched hands of Splinter Danaher and roared past, that rolled and rolled on to deep center with the two Cards in hot pursuit. While Bob Russell romped across with the winning run.

The fans were on the field, mobbing the players. They caught Hathaway before he could get back from second base; they pulled at his sleeves and slapped him on the back, while the team stuffed their gloves in their pockets and ran in triumph for the clubhouse. Old Fat Stuff stood before the bench watching the scene.

"Yes, sir, I told you he'd go and do something like that. The best way to get along with Bones Hathaway at the platter is not to go chucking at his noggin. I knew he'd clout one after that duster, I sure did. Good work there, Bonesy, you sure delivered that time . . . and now, boy, bring on them Yanks!"

John R. Tunis (1889–1975) was considered one of the finest writers for boys during the 1940s and 1950s. He played collegiate sports at Harvard, served in World War I, and after the war worked as a sportswriter and commentator, publishing articles in popular magazines such as *The New Yorker* and *The Saturday Evening Post*. It wasn't until 1938, when he was forty-nine, that he wrote the first of his more than twenty books for young people. That novel, *Iron Duke*, won the *New York Tribune*'s Spring Book Festival award, and many of his later novels were also award winners. Mr. Tunis's knowledge of sports, his attention to detail, and his concern over social issues give his novels a timeless relevance and appeal that have made them enduringly popular with readers of all ages.